# Secrets of the Bayou

by Alice Lunsford

**DORRANCE**
PUBLISHING CO
EST. 1920
PITTSBURGH, PENNSYLVANIA 15238

Dorrance Publishing Co
585 Alpha Drive
Suite 103
Pittsburgh, PA 15238
Visit our website at *www.dorrancebookstore.com*

ISBN: 978-1-4809-2514-4
eISBN: 978-1-4809-2284-6

# *Chapter One*

The room and its occupants waited patiently for their victim, the tomb-like blackness of the room muting sounds that penetrated less sturdy walls. No preparation was made to lure the unsuspecting visitor, no brass band, no red carpet, because one day the guest would arrive and promises would be kept.

No other guests were welcomed in the room as beleaguered hotel managers came to realize after countless complaints from indignant overnighters objecting to sleep deprivation from 'strange noises' and 'funny shadows'. Disturbances reached out like an insidious London fog intimidating those who shared the second floor. One day drapes were drawn for the last time and that floor was 'closed for repairs'.

Permanently. No one wished to share a room with ghosts.

The door to room 209 was opened only occasionally to allow perfunctory cleanings by hasty maids, after which the disturbed dust settled back into place and the frightened women scuttled back to the depths of the old hotel to whisper of unseen terrors. And the unearthly wait began again.

*The Mamba had a snake called Zombi which could bring sickness or death, good or bad luck, life or death.*

*The people of Bayou Vieux were afraid of the mamba and her snake. She would drape it around her shoulders and shake and twist herself in time to the drums while those dancing around the fire would roll their eyes till only the whites showed, then fall to the ground, hissing like Zombi.*

*The rituals had begun.*

"But you haven't given me one freaking reason why you won't go out with us!"

Beach-bound and feisty, Corky's chirp showed a higher level of petulance than usual as she puffed through the morning's mail, her tanned curves snug in a striped tank top and bleached cut-offs.

Down the hall in a tiny bathroom where potted plants engulfed sink, tub, and toilet, Karen Benoit studied her turban-wrapped head in the mirror and wondered once again why she had agreed to share three rooms with a burgeoning actress. And got the usual response: the money, honey. A decent Santa Monica apartment with a sliver of an ocean view could not be bought for a one-woman song and dance - even if she had the flair.

"I told you," she said, dripping into the living room and salvaging the *LA Times* from the four corners of the room, "seven-foot basketball players aren't my type."

"Neither are six-foot biochemists or anyone else who could show you a good time," her roommate muttered, skimming over the latest lecture from her mother. "You could get any guy you want. Look at that chick." She pointed to a newspaper photo of a blonde model rolling around the sand with a beach ball. "You could be her double."

"Sure - with face lifts and liposuction. Have a good time last night?" Karen removed a bra from under a cushion on the splashy red and purple sofa. The end tables were littered with lipstick-stained glasses and beer bottles. Useless to tidy with Corky's talent for clutter.

"He-do-nis-tic! Hey, Karen, here's something for you, and it's not a bill." Corky held out a pale, blue envelope.

"You're kidding. Sure it's not for you?"

"Oh, take it! I knew you had a past."

Karen stared at the spidery scrawl. "I can't read the writing; it's too faint."

"Give it here." Corky grabbed the fragile envelope and squinted as she read: "'Zelena D'Aquin, Vencus Plantation, 1007 Loop Road, Bayou Vieux, Louisiana' What a name! Who is she? Some rich relative?"

"Can't say, I never heard of her."

"So open it!"

"Maybe later."

"Oh, for Pete's sake, you're always complaining you don't have a family."

Just once, Karen thought, remembering an evening when, awash with self-pity and wine she told Corky of her history of foster homes. She had since regretted the maudlin confession as Corky now looked upon her as the poster child for unwanted beings.

She hesitated before slitting open the envelope, then stared at the extraordinary words, not quite comprehending them. A faded photograph fell to the floor.

"Well? What does it say?" Corky scooped up the picture of two little girls in a rowboat. "Who are they? They look like twins."

Karen walked out onto their microscopic balcony and gazed at the spindly palm trees, tiled roof tops and labyrinth of telephone wires. This couldn't be; she had waited too long for some sign she was not alone. The years spent dampening her pillow with tears shed for someone who would never come were long gone. This letter was someone's poor idea of a joke.

Corky followed her, squeaking with excitement. "This is it, right? You're getting rich from some long, lost relative?"

Karen kept her back to Corky, unwilling to shed tears in front of her nosy roommate.

"Don't be ridiculous."

"But what does it say? Give it here, girl!"

Corky snatched the thin sheet of paper before Karen had a chance to stop her.

"Shit, your aunt must be 112 years old, I can barely read her writing." Corky read aloud in a quivering old lady's voice: "'My dear Karen: This must seem a voice out of the past to you, if you remember me at all. I apologize for not contacting you sooner. I am your mother's sister and very anxious to meet you again, so we may resume the loving relationship we once had. I know you probably want to learn more about the mother you never knew, and I am prepared to tell you all you wish to know. I would like you to visit us at Vencus Plantation starting April 2 for five days when my husband and I will be celebrating a very special anniversary. Please call me at 335-334-9289 or respond by letter to Vencus Plantation, 1007 Loop Road, Bayou Vieux, Louisiana. Looking forward to hearing from you, Sincerely, Zelena D'Aquin.' Cool. When you going to call her?"

Karen quietly retrieved the letter and picture and slipped them back into the envelope, aware of the faint scent of lavender that lingered in the air from the note paper. She looked down on the promenade below at two young girls on skates who almost collided with an old man in a wheel chair. Oblivious to his shouts of rage, the pre-teens looked to be the same age as the two girls in the photograph.

"Karen? Did you hear me? You *are* going, aren't you?"

"Of course not."

"Why the hell not?"

Karen spun around, suddenly furious at this fun-loving Barbie-doll pestering her to take an action that quite frankly repulsed her. Corky probably never had a bleak moment in her life, having been raised by doting parents who pampered every waking instant of her precious life.

"Why's she writing now?" Karen demanded. "All my life I believed my mother died when I was born and that I had no other relatives. Now I'm supposed to believe this sentimental drivel? I don't think so!" She tore the tissue-thin envelope in half while angrily watching the tranquil scene below. Myriads of tiny white specks dotted a slim blue patch in the distance. The marina was waking up; hundreds of weekend sailors were taking advantage of the good weather.

"Now I *know* you're nuts," Corky muttered, retrieving the torn pieces of paper before they were blown away by a capricious breeze. She marched back into the living room and pieced the letter and photo together on the coffee table. "Cute girls, they look like you." She scanned the note. "An anniversary party. Isn't that romantic? How long do you suppose your aunt's been married? It doesn't say."

"Since I never heard of her 'til this moment, I can't imagine. By the look of the handwriting I'd say a hundred years."

"I wonder if this one's your aunt. You gotta go, Kar! She said she was sorry she never contacted you. Maybe she had amnesia."

"For fifteen years? Don't they have doctors in -" Karen glanced at the envelope, "-Bayou Vieux?"

A rat-a-tat-tat at the door prevented further arguments.

"Last chance to go with us, honey. This guy's a real hunk, and every one of his buddies are sexy as hell. You can't stay locked up in this cell forever."

"I appreciate your concern, Corky, but I told you before I'm not interested in one-night-stands."

Corky shrugged and grabbed her purse. "You don't know what you're missing, babe!" She flung open the door and threw her arms around a tanned muscle-bound Neanderthal with bleached hair. "You make that call, girl!" she trilled over her shoulder. "We'll talk later."

And Corky and her latest toy were gone.

Sleep came late and fragmented that night. Corky never came home and Karen read the night away, hoping she could rely on Jane Austen as her sure-fire cure for insomnia, but for some reason the novelist had become fascinating reading at 2 am. Frustrated, she shoved *Pride and Prejudice* into the drawer of her night stand deciding Elizabeth and Mr. Darcy could do without her at this pre-dawn wake-a-thon, and let her thoughts ramble uneasily down old, familiar paths.

Life alternated between the security hi-rise Karen called home and a minuscule cubicle in Century City where she daily wrote volumes of greeting card pap. After six months at "Joy's Prose," she could turn out sappy jingles faster than the average reader could read. She met Corky at a Starbucks where they had laughed over the would-be actress's adventures as a giant chicken while waiting for stardom. Corky wanted someone to share the rent. Why not? Karen decided - better than the Gordons, Taylors and all the other disagreeable families who had housed her for the past twelve years. Karen and Corky became self-sufficient roommates and surface friends - the only kind Karen could tolerate. Her more lasting companions were found on library shelves.

When sleep finally claimed her, Karen dreamt about two little girls giggling and exchanging secrets as they cruised a water-lily-clogged bayou on a sunny day. Suddenly, the sky and water turned ink-black, then crimson as if the banks of the swamp were on fire. An egret flew against the threatening background then settled on a lily and sank gracefully into the still water. When the egret disappeared, the bayou metamorphosed into a dark closet, and Karen found herself clawing at the walls of the closet, screaming in vain for help. She awoke terrified, wondering what chunk of her life had been exposed by an invitation to visit a place she'd never heard of.

# Chapter Two

The next night, as the girls relaxed over a glass of wine - Corky, dateless for a change, and Karen taking a breather from her endless non-literary scribbling—Corky momentarily took her eyes off the television screen to focus on Karen. "Did you call?"

"I did not. I told you, I'm not going."

"Wimp! You'll never take a chance that just maybe there might be something good out there."

"I've got too much work to do. *Someone's* got to pay the bills." (A reference to Corky's folks' failure to send last month's check.) "Besides, I've got to work on the new line of Christmas cards."

"In *February* for God's sake? I just got around to throwing out last year's."

"Those people don't want me. They never cared about me before, how'd they find me now?"

"We *are* in the 21st Century. All she had to do was Google you. Where's that letter? You didn't throw it away, did you?"

"Hadn't got around to it."

"Well, don't!" Corky refilled both glasses then flounced over to the table and picked up a piece of the torn letter. "Now call!"

"Stop hassling me, bully!" After two and one half glasses of Merlot, Karen had no intention of being ordered about.

"Call, or I'll burn your books!"

Karen snatched Corky's address book from the desk. "Great! Start with yours!"

Corky groped in her purse for her cell phone and shoved it at Karen. "Call!"

"How can your parents stand you?"

"They love me! Someday I'll be their bread-and-butter. *Please?* You'll be happy you did, I promise!"

Karen drained the glass. "Oh, all right! What's the damn number?"

Corky squinted at the tiny piece of paper. "Hard to read after all that wine."

Karen chortled and dialed. The girls held their breaths for half a dozen rings until an irritated voice spoke into the phone. "Hello."

Karen was stunned into silence by the unexpected response until Corky rammed her with her elbow. "Talk, girl!" she hissed.

The voice repeated itself, louder and angrier this time. *"Hello!"*

Corky was making faces and unintelligible sounds at Karen. Giddy from wine and the effort of reaching out to the unknown, she shushed her roommate and steadied her voice. "May I speak to-" she glanced at the paper - "Mrs. Zelena D'Aquin, please?"

*"Sleeping!"* the irate voice said, and hung up.

Karen looked at her watch. "Good Lord, Corky, it's midnight there! Why'd you make me call her so late? The woman's sound asleep. You are *such* a bad influence!"

"Serves them right for being three hours later than us." She poured the rest of the Merlot into Karen's glass. "At least the internet stays awake when it's supposed to," she said, turning on the computer.

*"Now* what are you doing?"

"Where's that letter? You better get some Scotch tape, girl, or you're not going to have an address left to see. Don't you want to know what Vencus Plantation looks like?"

"You're too much!"

But they both watched in awe as a mansion out of *Gone With the Wind* appeared on the screen.

"My God, Karen, you're rich!"

"It's a relic from the Civil War."

"It says it used to be open for tours every spring during 'Plantation Days', then closed in 1998. Wonder what happened then?"

"With my luck, a plague."

"Built in 1790 - *wow* - the father of the present owner was a Superior Court Judge of Louisiana. You're not only rich, you're friggin' famous!"

Corky pressed more keys.

"And you're spying on *what* now?"

"We gotta check out this Bayou Vieux town. I never heard of it."

"Considering you never heard of Louisiana before this letter came, I'm not surprised."

"Shit, Karen, wine makes you downright nasty. Or maybe it's this new found power of yours. See there? 'Ten miles north of New Orleans' - honey, you have *got* to go now and take me with you - 'used to be big trade and political center, today a small town surrounded by a few plantations that weren't burned to the ground during the Civil War.' Those mean ol' Yankees!"

"Sounds interesting."

"Not as much as Vencus. Karen, you call that filthy rich aunt of yours tomorrow. I've gotta get some shuteye. I've got an audition Saturday morning for Pampers." At Karen's look - "I know, I know, but it'll buy me a new car if I get it."

"And I have a few more sappy cards to write for birthdays."

"Then you'll do *what* tomorrow?"

"I'll call, I'll call. Now shut up and go to bed."

Corky laughed and took the rest of the wine to bed with her.

After a moment, Karen sighed and took out a roll of Scotch Tape from the kitchen drawer.

The next morning, after her optimistic roommate skipped out of the apartment in a powdery white wig and a granny dress, Karen held an imaginary phone conversation with the woman who might possibly decide her future.

After a lengthy rehearsal and three cups of coffee, she dialed the phone number listed in the invitation - and sat down suddenly when a voice several octaves higher than yesterday's glum respondent said, "This is Zelena D'Aquin. To whom am I speaking?"

Swallowing rapidly, Karen blurted out, "Karen Benoit in California. You wrote to me, asking me to visit you." The words ran down as quickly as her confidence as the silence on the other end of the phone lengthened.

This was a hoax, and a rotten one at that. She was about to hang up when the high, firm voice responded, "Excuse me, my dear, I'm quite overcome. I didn't dare hope you'd answer my letter."

Karen waited. This was no hoax; she could hear the emotion in the other woman's voice.

"Are you there, Karen? You haven't hung up, have you? Please let me know if you're still there."

"Yes, Mrs. D'Aquin, I'm here. I just wondered what this was all about. I wasn't aware I had an aunt."

"Oh, yes, my dear, you're my sister's only child, and I need to talk to you about your mother before it's too late."

"Is she all right?" Karen's voice faltered at the thought of suddenly losing the mother she'd never known.

"Oh, dear, I said that all wrong, I didn't mean to get your hopes up. Your mother died years ago. I just meant that I wanted you to come and visit your uncle and me. Vencus is quite lovely in the spring. You must stay with us for a few days while we get acquainted. I'll show you around this ridiculously small town and tell you all about your dear mother. Please say yes, Karen, I would be quite devastated if you turned me down."

"Well-" Karen hesitated, part of her yearning to hear more, the other half hiding behind the self-protecting barrier set up years ago.

"I'll take that as a yes." The woman's voice became firmer, more confident. "I'll send exact dates and directions immediately. I'm afraid I don't have a computer so you'll have to wait for another old-fashioned letter - and I'll send your airline tickets as well. You can't say no, Karen, you would break my heart." The line went dead.

What the hell! Pushy broad, Karen thought as she opened a new bottle of wine to contemplate the astonishing events of the last twenty-four hours. At least she'd have a free trip out of it - even if it was to the state she'd tried for years to leave.

UCLA was teeming with blue-robed graduates, balloons and gushing parents. Bo Boudreau felt a rare rush of loneliness as he dialed his parents back in Louisiana. He could picture his dad and all his non-working brothers huddled around the wall phone waiting for his call. His mother would be stirring a celebratory jambalaya in a giant pot on the old fashioned stove and a bevy of pecan and sweet potato pies would be cooling on the window sill. It was 3:00 pm by the time 10,000 seniors and another 1,000 graduate students - Bo included - finished parading across the stage with their diplomas, and 6:00 pm in Bayou Vieux. One ring was all it took for tee Sharle to answer the phone. His squeaky twelve-year-old voice came over loud and clear.

"Dat you, Bo?"

"Oui, Sharle, c'est moi."

Massive noises floated through the line. Bo shouted to get his brothers' attention but knew it was futile, they'd get back to him in their own sweet time.

"Sharle! Henri! Get mama on the phone!"

More scuffling, then a new voice. "Bo? Dis be Ulyssess. Ca viens?"

"Doing just fine, Ulyssess. How's LaLa?"

"She tired of waiting, Bo. Dat bébé be here any day now, fuh shore. When you be at here?"

"Tell her to wait a little longer, she can't have that bébé without me, you know that. Put mama on."

Another long pause, more scuffling and laughter. Bo's mother hated the phone, but loved Bo. He heard a soft sigh from the person responsible for making sure he graduated today. Finally he heard her tentative: "Vomment ca vas, cher?"

"Fine, Mama, just fine."

"You got you a chouchoo, heh?"

"It's called a Doctorate's Degree, Mama. And merci pour la cheque," he added.

"Buy you joli threads, Bo."

"Books, Mama, more books. Clothes come later."

"When you be here, cher? Papa got him a big ol' gar he say need skinning."

"Soon, Mama. Put papa on, okay?"

"Mais, non, Bo, dat couyon still be boude with you. He ain't gonna talk till you get here - if den," she added gloomily. "Me, I got you some good jambalaya and gumbo when you get here, Cher."

"Terrific, Mama, I'll be there 'bout this time tomorrow."

"Bon!" She started to hang up.

"And Mama, tell papa I was valedictorian, okay?"

"Dat be good or bad?"

"Dat be ver good."

"Me, I tell him, Bo, but you know dat bracque homme. Alex, he be thinkin' fancy college be only good for rich and mal gens."

"Hug papa for me, Mama, je t'aime."

He could hear her blow her nose as she muttered, "Moi aussi, Cher" and hung up.

# Chapter Three

Flight 114, non-stop to New Orleans, was almost full as Karen sat in window seat 23E, her mind as chaotic as the faces of her fellow passengers shoving uncompromising carry-ons into bulging overheads already crammed with tennis rackets, backpacks, enormous suitcases meant for the plane's baggage compartment, and other lop-sided packages filled with unnecessary gifts never to be used. For all the loading frenzy, there was an amazing amount of cheerful faces streaming on the plane - sure sign of happy vacationers.

She grinned at the sight of the empty seat beside her; she could spread out, read a book, knit a quilt (not that she wanted to) - or take a nap.

She stuck a squat, white pillow behind her head and fumbled in her tote bag for *Jane Eyre*. A romantic at heart, Karen looked forward to a good four-hour cry over the unrequited love of Jane and Mr. Rochester.

Two minutes before take-off, a mop of curly black hair topping a torso that rivaled any Q magazine centerfold sprinted down the aisle straight for Karen, now seriously caught up in her tragic tale. As the whirlwind neared, Karen looked up and observed with dismay a smiling face bronzed by hours in the sun. Golf or tennis pro she sniffed, and returned to her book.

"Sorry," said the lanky traveler as he fell into seat 23F.

"For?" Karen murmured, not looking up from her book. She was determined not to let her privacy be invaded by someone Corky would consider a hunk.

"Crowding your space. You looked comfortable until I sat down."

"I guess an empty seat would be too much to hope for," she replied, reading the same paragraph for the fourth time.

The intruder stashed a lumpy backpack under his chair and stretched out legs too long to cross.

"I'd find another seat, but there aren't any, so looks like you're stuck with me."

"Lucky me."

"Since we're sharing seats for the next 2,500 miles, we might as well get acquainted. I'm Bo Boudreau." He held out his hand.

Karen sighed. So much for Mr. Rochester's passion for Jane. Why couldn't 23F be the same strong, silent type? "Karen Benoit."

"A good Louisiana name. You from the South?"

She thought ruefully of years spent in that hot, muggy land. "You might say so."

"Visiting your folks or here for Mardi Gras?"

"Mardi Gras?" Oh no, once again in the wrong place at the wrong time.

"Probably where half the people on this plane are headed."

"When is it?"

"Tuesday. Laissez bon temps rouler! New Orleans party time!"

"I'm meeting relatives, so I won't have time to party."

"Ask them to show you around." His grin exposed gleaming teeth against chestnut-colored skin.

Karen stared pointedly out the window at a world of white cotton candy, her back a turn-off to all but the truly insensitive. He took the hint.

"Go ahead and read. Charlotte Brontë needs solitude."

She turned and regarded him thoughtfully. The Brontës weren't easily digested by bronzed Lotharios. "You like the Brontë sisters?"

"Charlotte Brontë brings out the romantic soul in me." When he shifted, his shoulder touched Karen's. To her annoyance, she felt her cheeks redden, and was grateful that her seatmate's attention was focused on the patient flight attendant's attempt to teach bored passengers the correct way to escape death if the plane fell.

"*Jane Eyre* probes every emotion there is," seat 23F continued thoughtfully, eyes on the attendant. "Love, vengeance, passion - Brontë could really play the heart strings." Bo's gaze shifted to Karen and she couldn't remember ever seeing such dark, piercing eyes - a startling resemblance to Charlotte's hero.

He fell silent, respecting her need for privacy. She suddenly wished she had Corky's flair for small talk.

The plane lurched, sending *Jane Eyre* skittering down the aisle. A matronly attendant stooped to pick up the book, then dove headfirst into Bo's lap when the plane bucked again. Several passengers snickered at the sight of the hapless woman struggling to extract herself while the plane went through a spasm of shimmies and bumps. The red-faced woman finally righted herself and handed Karen her book. "Thank you," Karen murmured, embarrassed to be the center of attention. The attendant then teetered from one side of the aisle to the other back to her seat.

"It helps to hold on to someone," Bo said as he pried Karen's white knuckles from the armrest and held her clammy hand in his cool one. "We're crossing the Mojave Desert and sometimes winds kick up down there."

Hating her wobbly voice, Karen stammered, "You f-fly this r-route often?"

"More, now that Lala is having her baby."

It wasn't the plane's shaking that dropped Karen's stomach to the floor.

"Your w-w-wife is having a b-b-baby?"

Bo laughed. "My *sister* Lala is having her first child, and she's doesn't act like much more than one herself."

His *sister.* Karen's voice settled back to normal. "How old is she?"

"Sixteen."

"Tough. Is she going to keep the baby?"

"You bet. She's been wanting one ever since she and Donny Bob got married last year."

Karen tried not to show her disapproval. Southern girls were considered outcasts if not married by eighteen. She changed the subject. "Where are you from?"

"Place called Bayou Vieux."

"But that's where *I'm* going! I'd never heard of the place till last week."

"I'm not surprised, it's barely on the map. Maybe we can get together while you're there."

"Oh, I don't think -" Karen started to say when the turbulence stopped. She tried to reclaim her hand, but her fellow passenger held tight.

"No sense letting go. These rocky winds can crop up again."

"If you say so," she said dryly. "Is Lala your only sister?"

"The only *pregnant* one right now. I have three sisters and five brothers. Cajuns like big families."

"You're Cajun?" He might as well have said Martian.

"A lot of Louisiana is. "

"So why are you coming from -" the plane shook again - "L - Los Angeles?"

"Just got my Doctorate from UCLA."

"Congratulations! Film school?" He was handsome enough to be in the movies.

"Neurology."

Smart, too. "I'm impressed. Will you practice in Louisiana?"

"Yep. See if I can find the cure for loup-garou."

"Loup what?"

"Garou. Aka werewolves. Superstition runs wild in Cajun country. Folks still believe in werewolves, vampires, zombies, voodoo."

So much for the intellect of her traveling companion. "We don't have werewolves in Santa Monica, but if I run into any I'll send them on." She eyed her imprisoned hand. "Are we safe now?"

"Always were. Just a tad bumpy for a while." He released her hand.

They rambled on about his studies, her boring job, their mutual love of Gothic novels, his talent for Cajun cooking, her ignorance of it, his large family, her non-family (without mentioning the twelve foster homes) and then the plane landed at New Orleans Airport with neither taking a further look at *Jane Eyre* or *Brain Diseases and Their Causes* jutting out of Bo's back pack. They agreed it was the fastest plane ride they'd ever taken, exchanged cell numbers, made tentative plans for a bayou picnic then said goodbye when the plane touched down. Karen was convinced they'd never see each other again.

"Hope ya'll have a good time while you're in N'awlins," drawled the busty blonde at the Rent-A-Car counter, handing Karen keys to a shiny white Toyota. "Guess you came for Mardi Gras. Hey! Watch it, Mister!" she yelled as a pirate reeking of beer crashed into Karen then staggered away. "Clods, ya see 'em everywhere. Mardi Gras's fun, but sometimes I wish the damn thing would hurry and get over with."

The airport was a riot of costumed revelers: gypsies, zombies, ghouls.

"Hey, sugar, give your lover a big smack!" Blue Beard was back, lifting Karen off her feet and spinning her around until she almost hit an enraged matron whose flailing umbrella missed the drunkard and thwacked Karen on the shoulder instead.

"I said quit it, Clyde!" Miss Rent-A-Car yelled, giving Bluebeard a fierce clip behind his neck which caused Karen to be dropped quicker than a sack of wildcats.

"Aw, baby, you don't fight fair. Where's all that Southern hospitality I heard about?"

"Sober up, and you'll find out."

He stumbled toward a nearby bar, rubbing his neck peevishly.

Miss Rent-A-Car handed Karen a lethal looking hat-pin embellished with a plastic pelican. "Don't be afraid to use this, dahlin' - souvenir of N'Awlins. You're gonna need it durin' Mardi Gras."

Karen yammered thanks and pushed toward the parking lot. As she groped her way through costumed tourists out for a good time, she wondered what had possessed her to go to Bayou Vieux, and why she hadn't bothered to check the holidays. Around her swirled every state of inebriation, with the exception of six Japanese schoolgirls whose guide led them past a riotous conga line headed by four hefty nuns. The fact that the nuns could all use a shave was a dead give-away to their sex. An odor of stale beer permeated the airport, and Karen stepped over puddles of water clogged with a week's worth of revelry.

When she finally reached the miniscule Toyota which would be hers for the next few days, she tossed a suitcase into the trunk, eased herself into the driver's seat, and studied the map of New Orleans and the surrounding countryside. Bayou Vieux - a dot one-eighth of an inch off the main highway - would be easy to find in the two hours before dusk. She picked up speed once she was on the deserted highway going away from New Orleans. Graceful strands of silvery moss shrouded huge oaks lining the road, a calming sight.

The car rounded a bend and Karen caught her breath at the sight of an eerie swamp that suddenly materialized before her. Murky clouds had overtaken a slowly sinking sun, and the still, dark water looked ghostly with forests of towering cypresses ringing the shore in one continuous green-black wall, its denseness broken only by masses of wispy moss. She parked by the side of the road, reached for her camera and got out of the car, careful not to slam the door which might startle a solitary heron standing in the water on one stick-like leg. Still, the snowy mass of feathers rose abruptly and glided off into a jungle of twisted cypresses and oaks, its mournful cry alerting hundreds of roosting snipes and grackles that lined the marsh. Squawking clouds of birds crowded the sky, then flew off to less people-inhabited bogs. The ghost forest settled down once more. Her eyes adjusted to the grey-green environment where giant blue and copper-colored irises danced on delicate stems, shadowing masses of flowering hyacinths. She shivered in the gathering dusk, wishing she had thought to bring a sweater.

The enchantment of the past few moments vanished as Karen almost drove through the main street of Bayou Vieux without realizing she was in the slowly decaying, two-hundred-year-old town.

On the outskirts of town, almost as an afterthought, was a well-kept cemetery. She parked near the entrance and exited the car, planning to sneak a quick look then continue on to her aunt's home. Half-a-dozen benches surrounded a gazebo where, according to a weathered announcement, Zydeco bands with names like 'Gator Bait' and 'Jumpin' Frog Louie' had played at last summer's concerts. Graves shaped like pyramids and miniature castles, adorned with angels and eagles, stood further back from the road, partially obscured by giant oaks and weeping willow trees.

Beyond the park, a three-story hotel of indeterminate age loomed up out of the twilight. The glow of lights on the first and third floors indicated that Mardi Gras visitors had overflowed to the suburbs of New Orleans.

Curiously, the hotel's second floor was dark.

According to the map, Loop Road was a block past the cemetery, and lack of street lights along the winding road made the approaching darkness seem ominous. Then she saw the graceful mansion set back in a tangle of vines and leafy oaks. Greek ionic columns supported a massive slanting roof which topped two stories. A verandah ran the length of the second floor, and two enormous wings flanked the main structure.

Karen parked the car and walked up half-a-dozen broad steps leading to the front entrance. There was no outside light, odd since she was expected. She rapped briskly with a wolf-shaped door knocker attached to the ornately carved door, triggering an explosion of menacing snarls and growls on the other side. She wondered if she could make it to her car before being torn to bits if the beasts managed to break through.

A sharp "Quiet" silenced the uproar, and a dark-skinned, heavy-set woman opened the door.

No dog was in sight.

# Chapter Four

The small wooden cabin overflowed with Boudreaus - all born and bred within the sturdy, water-stained walls - when Bo strolled in, laden with presents, especially for new-borns. After masses of noisy kisses and hugs, the family crowded around the long wooden trestle for a feast of turtle soup, boudin, étouffé and sweet potato pie - food Bo never got on campus. Talk was non-stop as each sibling did his or her best to tell the honored guest loudly what *they* were doing while he was frittering away life at UCLA. Only Bo's mother listened carefully as he tried to explain the ins and outs of college life, but soon her eyes glazed over, overwhelmed by lab talk and scientific terminology. His father was more to the point.

"Damn books! Can't make no livin' readin' damn books ou cuttin' up frogs - 'lessen you be gonna eat 'em!"

"The books will come in handy when I hang out my shingle, Papa."

"Bah, et where dat be at? Some fancy town lak N'Awlins?"

"Not New Orleans, I'm going to practice right here in Bayou Vieux."

"What be dat you gonna practice, Bo?" his youngest brother snickered. "You don't play no 'ccordian ou gitar!"

"Hey, you've seen me pluck those strings," Bo protested laughing.

His father snorted. "Only ting dat boy know to pick is brains, since he be gone. You got you somethin' 'gainst trappin', boy?"

"Folks in Bayou Vieux need help just as much as anywhere else, Papa."

"Me, *I* need help, Bo," Ullysis chimed in. "Lala, she don't lak bein' alone come nighttime now her bébé be near. She be all de time hollerin' for me to stay home. I got me dat nighttime job at de hotel. You wanna go sit for me till dat baby come?"

"I guess I could do that. It's quiet over there, right? Good place to read?"

"Sept ans ain't 'nuff time to read, boy?"

"I'm still doing research, Papa. I'm going to help while I'm here, you know that."

"Vous gonna do beaucoup de *bullshit*, dat's what you gonna do!"

"Hey Bo," sister Angelina giggled, tired of the boxing match the evening had turned into. "You got you any good lookin' babe in California?"

"Matter of fact I *did* sit with a nice looking girl on the way out here, and I liked her - although I can't say the feeling was mutual. We might get together while she's here."

"Don't hold your breath," his sister laughed.

"Cain't do dat neither in dis stuffy place. Come on, te Charles, you get you gitar and play us nice song out on de porch." Bo's father rose stiffly from the table and pushed open the screen door. Bo's siblings followed their father out onto the porch.

"I'll help with the dishes, Mama."

"You go out dere et make you peace with you papa, Bo. He talk mean, but he be missin' you lak crazy, you better believe you dat."

"Hello," Karen began tentatively - the woman before her might have been a statue for her absolute stillness – "I'm Karen Benoit. Mrs. D'Aquin expects me."

The woman nodded brusquely and disappeared into the shadows of the mansion.

How inhospitable, Karen thought, these people had invited *her*; she had never heard of the D'Aquins until a few days ago. Struggling to control her temper, she stepped through the door into a lavish foyer which resembled a museum entrance. An enormous, cloisonné vase was perched atop a heavily gilded Louis XIV entry table, while a crystal chandelier that would have cost a lifetime of salaries dangled above her head.

Corky was right: her aunt was loaded.

Five minutes turned to ten, then fifteen while Karen waited, a slow burn settling in her stomach. She was ready to bid her illusionary aunt a furious farewell and break all speed limits back to the airport when the silent one returned.

"Miz D'Aquin, she got a sick headache. You wait in dat room and Mr. D'Aquin he come soon. I be called Odelia if you want anything," and the specter was gone, as noiselessly as she had appeared.

Vowing to wring her roommate's neck the minute she saw her, Karen opened the designated door and sank into the first high-backed Louis XIV chair she came to. Very uncomfortable.

Seething, she surveyed her surroundings. An intricately carved rosewood grand piano dominated one end of the forty-foot room; a huge mirror encased in gold filigree hung over a marble fireplace large enough to roast an elephant and another crystal chandelier composed of hundreds of shimmering droplets dangled from a Wedgewood medallion in the center of the high ceiling. The medallion's motif of chubby pink cherubs and rosebuds was repeated in the four corners of the enormous room. The furnishings could have been lifted from Versailles.

After a half-hour wait, during which time Karen's blood pressure nearly caused instantaneous combustion, Odelia returned.

"Dinner ready," she announced dourly, as if leading Karen to her execution.

"I'm not going to be eating alone, am I?" Karen shouted after the retreating back. After getting no reaction, she muttered, "Hell and damnation" and entered a dining room the size of Dodger Stadium.

Having eaten nothing since the plane's rubbery ham sandwich hours before, Karen decisively plunged a heavy silver spoon into the bowl of aromatic gumbo set before her - and dissolved instantly into a state of bliss. She hadn't tasted food this good since Corky's parents had treated the girls to High Tea at the Beverly Hilton.

By the time she reached the final course, a brilliant crème brûlée, Karen was ready to forgive all. She reasoned that her aunt absolutely wanted to see her but was too sick and didn't want to spread germs; her uncle had obviously been called away on business.

Or maybe not.

Then where *was* he? Odelia hadn't said *he* was sick, too.

As was usually the case back in Santa Monica, wine gave her a false bravado and the wine at dinner had been exceptionally energizing. At the moment she felt ready to rip Vencus apart with her bare hands in order to find the couple who had appeared to her out of the blue. She would *demand* to know *why* they had issued this strange invitation to visit their gloomy, opulent mansion.

She pushed her chair back from the table, stalked into the hall, and studied four closed doors. The lady or the tiger, she mused, and opened the first door to her right.

The shadowy room was lit by a dying fire in a small brick fireplace. The library, she surmised by the crowded book shelves lining the room. After her eyes adjusted to the dim room she realized she was not alone: a slight figure was hunched over in a wing chair by the fire. Staring at the flickering flames, the person seemed unaware of her presence.

"Mr. D'Aquin? Is that you? This is Karen Benoit. I waited for you at dinner, but you never came. Were you aware I was right down the hall from you in the dining room?"

The white-haired man slowly turned toward her, yet did not look up - would not meet her eyes. "I was busy," he said finally.

"And *Mrs.* D'Aquine? Was *she* too busy to meet me after I came all this way on her invitation?"

"My wife is not well. She informed me of her invitation to you."

"I was under the impression the invitation came from both of you," Karen said heatedly.

"Unfortunately that was not the case." Karen fidgeted, aware of yet another of life's inevitable setbacks. "If you wish, you may select something to read tonight from my library." D'Aquin fluttered a skeletal hand toward the stacks of books around the room. "There are quite a few first editions and portfolios - those are the only items I must insist remain in the room. Anything else you may take back to the hotel with you tomorrow."

Karen did a double take. "Hotel? But I was invited to stay here!"

"I'm afraid my wife was rather generous with her offer of hospitality - and forgetful. We are entertaining out-of-town guests beginning tomorrow and all our rooms will be taken. That is why I was rather perplexed when you arrived, and I didn't feel up to dining with you. Once again Zelena neglected to take me into her confidence. An oversight, no doubt."

"How embarrassing. I shall leave immediately."

"There is nothing with which to concern yourself. The St. Francis is quite respectable. Now, if you will excuse me, I have some work to do. Odelia will show you to your room and tomorrow my wife will acquaint you with our land of bayous and superstitions. If I'm not around you can easily find your way back to the hotel. Your room will be ready at noon."

After dropping this latest bombshell, D'Aquin left before Karen could question him further. Remembering the exceptional meal, she decided not to cause a scene - yet.

Much later, after Agatha Christy had dropped to the floor and Karen was twisting under an enormous four-poster canopy, she thought she heard someone crying in the hall. She switched on a night light, but the limited illumination cast only shadows around the dark bedroom. "Is someone there?" Karen called loudly, annoyed at this latest intrusion, yet concerned someone might need aid.

The crying stopped, followed by the soft padding of feet outside her door, like an animal pacing back and forth.

Unwilling to be torn to pieces by a maniacal dog in the middle of the night, she waited until the ominous sounds disappeared, then slipped out of bed and bolted the latch over the silver doorknob.

She groped her way back to bed and fell asleep immediately, exhausted by the uneventful, yet remarkable evening.

# *Chapter Five*

$\mathcal{T}$he next morning Karen drove back to the hotel she had previously seen only from a distance, past dense greenery hanging motionless along Loop Road, the foliage interspersed with broad stretches of emerald green lawns leading to graceful colonial homes - some well-cared for, others in ruins. The lush vegetation, sparkling in the morning sun failed to cheer her.

Apparently the D'Aquins were late risers, so, after a solitary breakfast, Karen had strolled the grounds of Vencus, surprised to see that Bayou Vieux wound past the back of the house at the base of a sloping hill. She walked along a daffodil-speckled path to the waterfront where the main attraction was a family of turtles sunning on the shore, then returned to Vencus only to be told her aunt was still sleeping and could not be disturbed. Her uncle had already left the house without bothering to see her.

Frustrated, Karen threw her suitcase into the trunk of the car and drove back to the small town. The previous evening had been anything but normal and the rudeness of Richard D'Aquin still smarted. She couldn't forget the late-night sobs outside her door. What if her aunt wasn't really sick but instead was being prevented from seeing her for some devious reason? Zelena D'Aquin had sounded normal on the phone two weeks ago, but perhaps that was a cover up for the woman's real fears. And now Karen was being chased out of Vencus without ever seeing her. Well, that wasn't going to happen, she decided. Her wistful yearning to belong was replaced by a determination to make sure nothing unscrupulous was going on at her so-called aunt's home.

The St. Francis Hotel was as hushed as the aftermath of a hurricane, which could well have happened by the look of the hotel, knee-deep in carnival debris. Heavy oak chairs and somberly patterned sofas were cluttered with confetti, streamers, discarded masks, food-encrusted paper plates, and torn paper hats making Venice Beach look like the Riviera on a sparkling day. Two cleaning ladies haphazardly shifted litter from one corner of the lobby to the other, overwhelmed by the tides of trash. Karen picked her way through the debris to the dozing clerk behind the counter.

Darker-skinned than either maid, the desk manager wore his white hair Afro style. Horn-rimmed glasses, a dark pin-striped suit and gray tie gave him a dignified appearance. Karen paused before tapping the bell, reluctant to wake the elderly gentleman. His head jerked up at the shrill ring. "Wha-what can I do for you, Miss?"

"My name is Karen Benoit. You have a room for me."

The old man's eyes widened as he stared at the ledger.

"Is something wrong? Don't I have a reservation? Richard D'Aquin said he made one for me."

The clerk cleared his throat, drummed his fingers on the counter obviously upset about something, then looked up from the reservation book. "Nothing wrong, Miz Benoit. Sign here, please." Was *everything* out of sync in Bayou Vieux?

"Must have been quite a party last night," Karen mumbled as she signed the registry.

"Yes, Miss, there be parties all over. We got 'nother tonight so you ought to get you a costume and come." He tapped the bell. "Tank take you to your room, Miz Benoit."

A boy about ten ran up to the desk, hitching his pants on the way, dark skin shining from tiny beads of sweat.

"Yessir, Miz Benoit, gonna be high time tonight." The clerk handed Karen a key.

"Thanks for the warning. I'll stay in my room."

"Then you be only one who do, Miz Benoit. I be here till noon today if you be needing something. Just ask for old Telemaque. Tank here be good boy; he be my grandson. Tank, you take dis lady up to room 309. You be lucky, Miss, gentleman who have room before you had too much good time. He wife took he home yesterday. It be only empty room all week."

"Best room in de hotel, ma'am," Tank said proudly, flinging open the door to 309. He set the suitcase in the center of a faded oriental rug, then strolled over to a pair of heavy velvet curtains and tugged at a thick braided sash. After a brief struggle, the boy won out and the drapes parted to reveal a wrought-iron balcony.

The high-ceilinged room was straight out of every Southern Gothic novel ever written. Cumbersome, dark furniture, water-stained walls papered in faded green, massive portraits of severe Confederate officers and haughty ladies spoke of gloom and by-gone generations. "Nice," Karen said, tussling with a door opening onto the balcony.

"Gotta do it dis way." Tank kicked the bottom half of the door while twisting the brass handle. The door creaked open and Karen stepped out onto a balcony considerably larger than the one she shared with Corky.

"Lovely view," she said to please the small boy who had worked so hard. "Yessum, if you like bone yards." He pointed to rows of white squares, their symmetry broken by lofty angels or obelisks. "You don't want to go dere at night, ma'am. Dat place be full of hants and zombies."

"I don't plan to go there at night."

He looked around the room and shivered. "Dey be other places, too, ma'am. Ghosts be ev'where. Some nights I hear 'em moaning so loud I can't hardly go to sleep."

"Oh, Tank, you don't believe in ghosts - a big boy like you? There's no such thing!"

"Tell dat to old Enzie Simon, ma'am, ev'body know he been robbin' graves for years. One night ev' hant in dat whole damn bone yard get up and walk over to he house on de bayou. Whole town seen 'em walkin' - dey say you ain't never heard such a clankin' and groanin' in your life. Old Enzie's house glowin' all night long from all dem spooks in dere. Next mornin' dey find he deader than dem what he used to rob, he hair be white as bones."

"That's just a story, you can't believe it."

"It be true as de devil's horns!"

"Were you there? Did you see it?"

"Not lessen Tank be one hundred and fifty years old!"

"It's not true. People try to scare kids with ghost stories. They think it's funny."

Tank dug deep into his pocket, bringing forth a handful of dirt. "Dis be grave dirt, ma'am. Carry dis stuff and ain't *no* spooks gonna get you." He held the dirt in the palm of his hand. "You want some? Old Telemaque get you more. He be braver dan Tank, you bet."

"A clump of dirt isn't going to protect me from something that doesn't exist."

The child pressed closer, surrounding Karen with pungent little boy odors of sweat and grime. "Lady, you watch out while you be here. I got dis and more gris-gris. *Good* gris-gris," he whispered, scooting into the hall before Karen could give him a tip.

Amused at the child's naivety, Karen unpacked the few clothes she'd brought and hung them in an ancient, mothball-scented armoire. Eager to explore the small town of Bayou Vieux, she stepped into the hallway, almost colliding with a beanpole of a man dressed as a monk.

"Bitch!" the monk yelled at a short, chunky person dressed as a nun.

"Bastard!" the nun retaliated, and the two swayed down the hall hurling obscenities at each other. Festivities had started early for them.

The haranguing continued to the elevator, the bickerers pausing only to drink from their Hurricane glasses. Karen glanced at her watch: eleven o'clock. No telling their condition by 11 that night.

The nun glared at Karen, then said in a deep voice. "How come you don't have no costume? Don'cha know it's Mardi Gras?"

Surprise! The 'she' was a 'he.'

"I didn't realize that when I was packing, otherwise I would have brought one," she lied.

"Pukey can give you something to wear if you don't mind being a clown. Everything that queen's got looks like it belongs in a circus!"

"Shut up, bitch! With the dough *you* make, I'm lucky to wear *anything*." Karen could think of a thousand places she'd rather be than in an elevator with two drunks. "I'm going to walk; it's taking too long," she said hurrying to the stair exit.

She had almost reached the second floor landing when a wave of dizziness flooded her senses; she sat abruptly on a step to avoid toppling over the banister. Her head felt drained of blood as she shivered and sweated at the same time. The landing was three steps away, yet she knew she'd pass out if she walked the short distance. Hunched over on the cold, cement stairs, she scooted toward the exit.

But the nausea increased and a sharp pain in her chest stopped her from going further.

A heart attack?

She regretted leaving her cell phone back in the room, but doubted if they had 911 in this backwater town. Mustering all her strength, she pulled herself to a standing position and stumbled to the door leading to the second floor.

The handle wouldn't budge. Sweat poured down her face, blurring her vision. *Locked!* The damn door was locked! Who the hell locked exit doors? She yelled for help repeatedly, shivering, waiting for the door to be opened. Nothing happened. No quick footsteps hurrying to the rescue, no calming voice saying the door would be unlocked in a minute. Was the entire hotel empty? Where were the two clowns she saw on the second floor? She shouted and pounded non-stop on the door for another minute than waited for what surely would be *some* response to the clatter she was making. In the stillness that followed all she could hear was the hammering of her heart and - laughter? Very faint, like a child's giggle. "Who's there?" she yelled. "Hey! You out there. Either unlock this door or go get someone who *can* unlock it! *Can you hear me?*" The laughter stopped, replaced by a silence heavier than before, as if someone was waiting for her next move.

Suddenly Karen was overwhelmed with the awful suspicion that she had imagined the laughter and that *no one* was going to let her out. If she were to survive this baffling attack, she had no other option than to use the stairs again.

As soon as she started toward the first floor the queasiness returned. To keep from falling she had to sit on the steps and ease her way down, biting her lip till it bled to block out the terrifying pain in her chest.

She was four steps from the bottom when suddenly the trembling and nausea vanished. No immobilizing pain, nothing but sheer relief that she wasn't going to die after all. She could walk, not crawl, and she fairly flew down the last four stairs. She burst into the lobby, thrilled to be normal again.

As she walked joyfully toward the front desk no one gave her a second glance. Surely she must look peculiar, paler than usual, maybe flushed from her ordeal. Her heart wasn't even beating faster than usual. Had no one heard her? Apparently not. Since she could find no explanation for her near-death experience, Karen chalked up the devastating event to just another show of southern inhospitality.

# Chapter Six

Telemaque was engrossed in a game of solitaire when Karen walked up to the desk. "This hotel has very thick walls," she said quietly, not wishing to startle the old man.

"Yes'um," he said absently, placing the two of hearts on the red ace.

"I'm sure it's against hotel rules to keep exit doors locked."

He looked up from his game with a quizzical look on his face. "Shouldn't be no doors locked, Miz Benoit."

"The one on the second floor was."

"I'll check it out, Miz Benoit."

"Thank you."

Platters of doughnuts, little cakes, a large bowl of popcorn and a dish containing pennies, nickels and dimes decked the counter.

"Looks like Trick or Treat, but this isn't Halloween."

"No, Miz Benoit. Mardi Gras. Masked riders come soon."

"'Masked riders'? Sounds dangerous," she laughed. "But they can't be if they're satisfied with doughnuts and pennies."

"Only dangerous if you *don't* give dem something. Dey part of Cajun Mardi Gras. You take you petite gateau, yes? It be real good."

"No thanks, I'm eating in the dining room. Popcorn looks good, though."

"Dat be 'tac-tac'. You stay in Cajun country; it be good you know dat."

"Tac-tac. I'll remember. Let me know if I get any phone calls, will you?"

A sign over the entrance to the dining room read: 'Mardi Gras Ball tonight. Zydeco!! Costumes!!!!' Karen walked into the almost empty room and did an abrupt turn when she saw the nun and monk in a corner. Too late, the combatants had spotted her.

"Yoo-hoo!" the nun hollered.

"Come sit with us!" the monk twittered. The two hadn't sobered up yet.

Karen glanced at her watch. "Oh, my, I am *so* late!" she cried, and made a quick spin back to the lobby. "Changed my mind," she murmured, to Telemaque, helping herself to a small purple, yellow and green cake. She dropped a few coins into the dish.

"No, no, Miz Benoit," he said, returning her change. "Money for riders. Gateau for free. We got chickens in kitchen also for riders."

"Lucky riders." She glanced at a newspaper rack which held two newspapers: *The New Orleans Times-Picayun* and *The Bayou Vieux Gazette*, which looked to be printed in someone's basement.

"Do you have the *Los Angeles Times*?"

"Ain't no fancy California newspapers here," Telemaque chuckled. "Down here folks like local stuff - Cora Mae's frog legs gumbo - stuff like dat."

"Sounds delicious." Karen said, removing the Gazette from the rack. "Don't forget my messages, will you? By the way, are there any gas leaks in the hotel? Something in the stairwell made me sick when I walked down from the third floor."

Telemaque glanced at the nun waddling out of the dining room, puffing a cigar. "We know soon enough if dere is, Miz Benoit. Dat cigar be big enough to set de Mississippi on fire."

"It sure is," she agreed. "They don't allow smoking in Southern California," she laughed, "no matter how religious you are."

She started for the front door.

"Watch out for de Zulus and Squa-tou-las, Miz Benoit," Telemaque called after her. "Dey get a mite out of hand, sometime. Dey means okay, though."

Karen turned back. "The Zulus and *what*?"

"If dey ask for chickens, send 'em here."

"If you say so," she said, walking out of the wacky, old hotel.

The skies were clear. Karen tucked the newspaper under her arm and followed the road to the cemetery, ignoring long, wet grass that clung to her ankles like snakes. What a relief to be out of that stuffy hotel. She hated staying five nights at the St. Francis, but had no other choice. The D'Aquins were anything but cordial, and she hadn't counted on masses of merrymakers disrupting her R and R.

When she reached the cemetery, she wiped dew from an iron bench and sat down to read about this land of gris-gris and tac-tac. The paper was all about Mardi Gras and what the Queen was going to wear at the Bacchus Ball - better than the latest gumbo recipe. The air was still save for the occasional croak of invisible frogs.

She was about to read about secret clubs called Krewes that dominated New Orleans social life, when she was startled by the sound of galloping horses and saw a fantastic assemblage racing toward her. Horsemen dressed like Indians banged on tambourines, pots and pans while children on foot, resplendent in Native-American garb, beat tattoos on drums and saucepans as they scampered to keep up with the adults on horseback. Bright sequins, brilliant beads and feathered headdresses presented a dazzling spectacle in the noonday sun. The riders were black, not a white face among them.

The parade halted in front of the hotel and the riders dismounted, tied their mounts to hotel pillars, and disappeared into the St. Francis. More mysteries. Where had they come from? The map indicated swampland the direction they rode from. Lake Ponchartrain was mostly wilderness to the northwest. Where ever the masked riders lived, they were a part of the vast pilgrimage invading New Orleans.

Wild whoops heralded their exit from the hotel a short time later, and the "Indians" leaped on their horses, while those on foot ran alongside, passing close enough for Karen to see the chickens they were carrying.

The procession halted outside the cemetery. The chief turned his horse to face the others, raised a hand and shouted "Tu-a-wa-pa-ka-way. The Indians are on the march today. Tu-a-wa-pa-ka-way."

The children repeated the chant in a high, sing-song chirp, then backed away as the adults spurred their horses and galloped away in the direction of New Orleans. After the horsemen left, the little braves ran back to the swamp or wherever they had come from.

Nothing like that in Santa Monica. Karen thought in amazement, and decided to go back to The St. Francis to learn more about the exotic group. Just as she was entering the building, a little girl ran out on a second floor balcony, to watch the disappearing parade. At the same time a giggling Scarlet O'Hara look-alike swept down the verandah stairs into a waiting car, distracting Karen as she stepped aside to let the Southern belle pass. When she looked back at the second floor, the child was gone and the balcony doors were closed, giving no indication of ever having been opened.

'Curiouser and curiouser,' to quote a favorite heroine.

The lobby was filling with costumed noisemakers, hell-bent on a good time. SpongeBobs and Spider Men dodged recklessly around the columns. A Superman crashed into Karen, entangling her with his enormous cape.

"I'm telling you for the last time, Leroy Humphrey, you sit down and behave or you ain't going to any parade!" shrieked an enormous woman in a tiny can-can costume. Pillows of flesh rolled out from the edges of her costume like inflated balloons. "Wish to hell your daddy would get on down here! It ain't safe for a decent woman to be alone at Mardi Gras!"

Karen would have gladly given her the pelican hat pin if she'd had it with her.

The sleepy, friendly face of Telemaque was gone, replaced by another dark-skinned man. Skin tones were the only similarity. Tinted glasses rested on the youthful clerk's short, straight nose, and partially concealed his high cheek bones. A thin smile revealed perfect, gleaming teeth.

"May I help you?" the new clerk asked in an educated voice which was in stark contrast to Telemaque's bayou drawl.

"I'm Karen Benoit, staying till Wednesday. Were there any phone calls for me?"

The clerk checked the mail slots, complaining aloud about the need for more updated equipment in a hotel which probably had never even seen a computer. "Nothing here, but I'll let you know if anything comes in."

Karen hesitated. The young man seemed so out of place with his buttoned-up striped shirt and skinny jeans.

"Was there anything else, Miss Benoit?"

"Not a thing - except I'm way out of my element in Bayou Vieux. I just don't understand this place."

He laughed. "I felt the same way when I moved here. Had to leave New York before it chewed me up."

"So what's it like here? Apart from being on another planet?"

"Which do you mean, the town or the hotel?"

"The boy who took me to my room was scared to death of ghosts. Is the hotel supposed to be haunted?"

"Rumors fly, but I've never seen or heard anything. Makes a good story." He handed her a pamphlet. "The St. Francis likes to advertise itself as "Louisiana's Most Haunted Hotel."

"Great, just what I need. And this is where my uncle stuck me."

"Your uncle?"

"Richard D'Aquin."

"The pot calling the kettle black."

"What's that supposed to mean?"

"You're talking about the D'Aquins at Vencus?"

"The same."

"Built by the same family who lives there now. One of the few plantations left standing during the Civil War. The mistress of the house was pregnant when the Yankees stormed Bayou Vieux and the captain had a soft heart for motherhood. Instead of burning the place down, he used it for a hospital. Lots of dead soldier boys running around dem dere hills today - or so the rumors go."

"Yikes! Maybe I'm better off here."

"Take your pick."

"What about Bayou Vieux?"

"Center of everything back then, but cotton growers didn't like the idea of railroads dirtying the precious fields my ancestors slaved on. Nearby Lafayette wanted the business so Bayou Vieux dried up. Now you see a town that decayed years ago. Perfect for a writer."

"Which I bet you are."

"You got it."

"How do you know all this?"

"Part of the training manual. Tourists love history and juicy stories."

"Figures. You know my name but I don't know yours."

"Lucius Bebar. Promise me you'll never call me anything but Lou."

"One more question, Lou, then I'll let you get back to work."

"I'm all yours. These Mardi Gras freaks are in their own little worlds."

"Those Indians that came in just now - really black men, weren't they?"

"Either the Golden Eagles, Creole Wild - Wests, or Wild Squa-tou-las. From the way they cleaned us out my guess would be the latter."

"Are they actually tribes?"

"In a sense. They're the black man's equivalent of white Mardi Gras krewes. Indians helped my ancestors escape in underground tunnels, so today African-Americans like to honor their benefactors by dressing up as them."

"Excuse me, *excuse me!* I've been trying to get your attention for the last half hour!" A woman with a face as red as the sash on her Mexican costume waved a pamphlet in Lou's face. "I want a swamp tour for tomorrow! Will you *please* take care of me *now?*"

"At your service, ma'am." Lou bowed extravagantly to the agitated woman.

"Thanks so much for the information, Mr. Bebar." Karen turned to the puffing woman and murmured, "I'm sure you'll love the tour; there shouldn't be too many alligators around this time of day," and left the distraught woman with mouth gaping.

She took the elevator to the third floor and walked the short distance to her room, surprised to find the door open.

The pretty young girl who earlier pushed debris around the lobby, was at the moment leaning over an open bureau drawer fingering Karen's good silk blouse.

"Can I help you?" Karen asked loudly.

The maid spun around, dropping the blouse to the floor. She made no effort to retrieve the silky material.

"Did you want something?" Karen repeated. Now she had thieves to deal with.

"No, ma'am - I just be cleaning, yes? I be going now."

"I don't see any cleaning supplies."

The girl eyed the door, measuring her chance of escape.

She wasn't getting away that easily. Karen stood in front of the door "What's your name?" she asked sternly. "In case I need something," she added hastily, not wishing to frighten off a possible source of much needed information.

The girl paused, then sniffed haughtily. "Dette. I be called Dette."

"I've never heard that name before. Is it short for something?"

"It be short for Odette. I be going now. Me - I got more rooms to clean," she mumbled, scurrying out the door.

Wondering why her relatives had subjected her to a haunted hotel *and* thieves, Karen picked up *A Murder Is Announced*, but couldn't concentrate; confused thoughts turned words into gibberish. The room grew dark, the sun swallowed by an army of advancing clouds. Soon a torrent of rain hammered against the French doors. She turned on the light above her head, determined to unravel Agatha's complicated story.

Hours crept by. At six PM, thoroughly frustrated by the lack of communication with her unsocial relatives, Karen ate a solitary dinner in a dining room slowly filling with happy revelers, then went back to her room. She'd been in Bayou Vieux for twenty-four hours now and still knew no more about her background then she did in Santa Monica.

A hot bath soothed her to the point where she no longer wished to throw a brick through the balcony doors. Dinner had been passable, the gumbo spicier than the D'Aquin's excellent concoction of shrimp, ham and chicken, and the wine was dry and crisp - not a bad break from writing cliché poetry.

She wrapped herself in a thick, oversized towel and stared into the bathroom mirror. Hot water matted her hair into stringy ringlets and her cheeks shone like overripe tomatoes - a far cry from the beach model Corky had compared her to. She dressed for bed and snuggled under the covers with her book. The patter of rain on the balcony added coziness to the night. She glanced at her watch – nine-thirty, still no call. Probably the old lady had recovered and sailed off to a ball in New Orleans. Useless to read - the plot was as indecipherable as Bayou Vieux so she got out of bed, opened the French doors and watched the gentle rain turn dingy graves into glistening marble monuments. A breeze ruffled her gown and she could smell the perfumes of a southern night - jasmine, magnolia, lilac. In the distance a fiddle played. Mardi Gras in full swing.

Suddenly, the loneliness she thought buried forever was back, as salient as the fiddler.

She closed the doors on the magical night and tried to untangle Miss Marple's mess.

# Chapter Seven

Karen was running for her life, her chest heaving as if it would explode from the exertion of the race - only she wasn't moving. Her feet were mired in the sludge of a Louisiana bayou and she was sinking into a pool of quicksand while all around her stirred a wilderness of ethereal beauty. White herons swooped and glided, floating in and out of mossy entrails dripping to the ground. One ghostlike bird settled in the midst of a giant, floating lily, then changed into a small child before sinking gracefully beneath the water. During the transformation the skies turned red, as if the swamp was on fire. If she could pull herself up by the long fingers of moss she could save herself and the child. She grabbed a dangling strand above her head, but the wispy vine became a snake. She let go of the twisting monster and the action forced her further down until finally the still, dark waters of the bayou closed over her head.

She awoke on sweat-dampened sheets and lay still, powerless to move. After the suffocating feeling gradually diminished, she felt a buoyancy as if surfacing from a watery grave, and fumbled for the night light. The soft glow was comforting, yet cast dark shadows around the unfamiliar room. As soon as her heart stopped racing she dialed O on the phone, frantic to hear a human voice.

"This is the desk. Can I help you?"

"Give me room service," she said, amazed at her steady voice.

"There's no room service between midnight and six AM."

"That's ridiculous!"

"Is something the matter?"

The voice was reassuring, vaguely familiar. "I'm having trouble sleeping and want a glass of milk."

"I can't be far from my desk but if you come down I can rustle up something from the kitchen."

"I'll be right down." Karen hung up, suddenly eager for human companionship.

The lobby was in semi-darkness with only a single light over the registry when she approached the man at the desk. "Thank goodness no one's here," she began, "I was afraid there'd be a room full of drunken -" She stopped, astonished to find herself staring at seat 23F from the plane.

"Hi, Karen. I saw your name and thought I'd surprise you."

"You certainly did - Bo, is it? What's a psychiatrist doing working in a hotel?"

"Being nice to my brother. He's the night clerk, but he doesn't want to leave his very pregnant wife alone at night."

"Lala. I remember." Karen smiled, suddenly happy to see a familiar face, "What a coincidence."

"It was meant to be. Let's go get that milk."

He led Karen into a large kitchen where accumulative odors of thousands of meals hung in the air, removed a carton from one of three refrigerators and poured the milk into a saucepan. "Take a seat, the milk won't take long to heat."

Karen sat in one of the chairs around the white enamel table. Anxieties of the past lessened as she watched Bo's easy manner.

"Every time I go to the lobby there's someone different behind the counter."

"You've met the last of us." He placed the cup of steaming milk in front of Karen and sat in the chair opposite her. "So here you are in my hometown. Have you seen your relatives yet?"

"Half of them. My aunt's sick so I've only met my uncle and that was briefly." She fell silent, chagrined at the memory of her treatment.

Sensing her discomfort, Bo was quiet a moment, then said gently, "What's their name? Maybe I know them."

"The D'Aquins. I suppose everyone knows everyone here."

"I know *of* them - big old house on the Loop, not exactly my league."

"Nor mine. I'm the poor relative."

"I wouldn't worry. Some rich folks have more problems than you'd want. Don't get me wrong, I'm sure your relatives don't fit that description. Want more milk?"

"If I do I'll fall asleep at the table, but it hit the spot."

"Stay awhile, everyone's still out whooping it up and you haven't lost that frog-jumped-in-your-gumbo look yet."

She smiled, relaxing in the warmth of his company.

"Want to talk about why you can't sleep? Although I warn you, I might try to analyze you."

"Might not be such a bad idea. My roommate says I need a padded cell."

"I've got all night."

That's all Karen needed. Before she could stop herself she had blurted out the whole story from the time of the invitation to the present. When she got to the panic attack in the stairway Bo frowned. "Let me know if it happens again, can't send you back to California in a basket."

"Probably just my over-active imagination."

"You're not pregnant, are you?"

Karen's mouth dropped open. "What kind of question is that? No, I'm not pregnant, and if I were, it'd be none of your business!"

Bo held up his hands in mock horror. "The lady's got a temper. Sorry, just trying to be funny, obviously failing."

"Obviously. Why'd you ask?"

"Just wondering if there was any truth to Cajun superstition. You said you dreamt of snakes. Sure fire way bayou folk know if they're pregnant."

Karen rolled her eyes. "How backward can you get?"

"I agree. But that stuff about Tank and gris-gris - be careful while you're here, sometimes things get out of hand."

"Oh, yeah, I'm supposed to take Tank and his cemetery dirt seriously."

"Not really, but swamp people grow up with this stuff."

"Well, *I* didn't, and someone should point out to them how ridiculous it is. That's what I'm here for, right?" She stood up, "Time for my nap."

He took her hand, and her mind raced back to the plane ride. "Hey, Karen, it's okay to lean on someone once in a while, but I get the feeling you never do."

She jerked her hand away. "You know nothing about me. Sorry I took up so much of your time."

His smile faded, and she regretted speaking so abruptly.

"No problem. Guess I better get back. Telemaque comes on at five and this place will be a zoo in an hour. Think you can sleep now?"

She nodded and left the kitchen, convinced she could. After talking to Bo, somehow ghostly swamps and dark stairwells didn't seem so sinister.

# Chapter Eight

A relentless sun beat through the undraped windows, waking Karen from a heavy, dreamless sleep. Eleven-fifteen. She dragged through the routine of toiletry, picked up the phone and dialed, determined to have it out with the woman who claimed to be her aunt.

After a dozen rings, a voice mumbled, "D'Aquin residence" into the phone.

Karen sat up straighter. "May I speak to Mrs. D'Aquin?"

"She can't come."

"This is Karen Benoit. Will you have her call me?"

"She be sick." The voice was final.

"May I speak to *Mr.* D'Aquin?"

"He be gone."

"Then let me speak to one of the guests. I want to leave a message."

"Ain't nobody here. Just me."

Karen struggled to keep anger from her voice, she was losing her temper much too frequently these days. "I need to speak to someone. Will my uncle and his guests be back soon?"

"Ain't no guests staying here."

"I thought they came in yesterday!"

"You thought wrong, lady." The phone went dead.

Instantly Karen dialed another number and counted ten rings waiting for Corky's sleepy voice.

"Yeah?"

"Hi, Corky, this is Karen."

"My God, how come you're waking me up in the middle of the night?"

"It's noon here. You should be up by now."

"Well, I'm not. Whadaya want?"

"I'm coming home. Will you meet me at the airport?"

"Hon, I'm not up 'cause I'm not going anywhere. L.A's shut down. We're floating into the Pacific! Five inches of rain in twenty-four hours and no signs of stopping. You'd be nuts to come home in this storm - probably no planes flying anyway. I thought your party wasn't till Tuesday."

"I'm not staying. My aunt refuses to see me, and they lied to me about having guests. They put me in a hotel."

"Why won't she see you?"

"Supposed to be sick."

"Yeah, well, a flu bug *is* going around."

"Corky, I'm 2,500 miles away."

"Okay, *okay*. Hang in there, kiddo, you've only got a few more days and then you can come home to sunshine."

"Why are you so evasive? Is someone in my bed?"

"Just till Wednesday, then he's got a dance job in Bakersfield."

"Didn't wait long, did you?"

"Don't be bitchy."

"I'm *not!* I just don't like strangers sleeping in my bed."

"You didn't know about Bobby when you called and you still sounded weird."

"This is a *weird* place, Corky - like I'm on some other planet. A lot of strange things are going on."

"Tell me about it when you get home; I'm beat and I gotta get some snooze time before Ricky picks me up. We're taking tango lessons, and I'll crash on the floor if I don't get a good sleep."

"Corky!"

"Just stay put and I'll pick you up Wednesday like we said. Find one of those cute Southern guys, and he'll keep you busy. They know how to push the right buttons. Can you hear the thunder? You're lucky to be out of this!"

The phone went dead. Good old Corky, always ready to help. Karen's growling stomach reminded her she hadn't eaten since six o'clock the night before. She dressed and went downstairs, determined to get questions answered as soon as possible.

Telemaque was shuffling cards when she went up to the desk.

"Are they still serving breakfast, Telemaque?"

"No, Miz Benoit, it be lunch time now."

"Sounds good. If any calls come for me, I'll be in the dining room."

After a crab salad spicier than Karen had in mind - Southerners had no restraint when it came to Tabasco sauce - she decided to walk to town. The February air was nippy so she went back to her room to get her jacket.

She stepped into the elevator and saw the nun - still in drag. She sighed and pushed the third floor button. The nun grunted and chewed an unlit cigar until the elevator stopped at the second floor. Karen stepped aside to let him out.

Icy claws ripped at her stomach. She felt the same revulsion as the day before. "You okay, lady? You look like you seen a ghost. You ain't gonna pass out on me, are you?"

"I'm okay." She wasn't going to be upset again. "Aren't you getting out?"

"Not me, lady, this is *your* floor."

"Not this floor."

"Then why'd you push the button?"

"*I didn't push the button and I don't want this floor!*" She was barely able to get the words out. "I want the third floor -"

"Make up your mind," he muttered and pressed the third floor button.

The doors closed with a jerk. The elevator lurched and wobbled upward. Stabbing sensations in Karen's stomach lessoned the further the car climbed, and by the time they stopped at the third floor the wretched feeling was gone. The fake nun wasted no time in getting out, and Karen stood for a moment in the hall, glad to be away from the stifling cage. *Was* there a gas leak on the second floor? If so, why had no one reported it? Why hadn't the man in the elevator noticed it? And why was no one staying on that floor? Too many unanswered questions. She remembered the child on the balcony. Something must have happened on that floor and they had moved everyone out to other floors. But Telemaque said she was lucky to get the only available room.

She was going in circles and going wacko in the process.

The phone rang just as she inserted the key in the lock. Zelena must be finally agreeing to meet her. Her hand trembled as she tried to unlock the door, and the phone rang on and on. Don't hang up, don't hang up, she muttered furiously as she twisted and jiggled the stubborn key.

At last the key turned and she threw open the door. "Hello?" she yelled into the phone.

A blast of wind pushed the French doors open. A whirlwind swept through the room, sending a vase smashing to the floor; papers and anything not anchored down cycloned around the room. A wispy scarf sailed through the air and draped over a corner of the mirror.

Stunned at the sudden tempest, Karen heard a click on the phone, then silence. Frustrated, she struggled to close the doors against the furious wind tangling her hair and clothes. Finally able to shut the doors, she caught sight of a wild woman in the mirror - herself. But not a leaf had dropped from the still trees on the lawn; not a breeze rippled the grass. The outside world was as peaceful as a Monet painting.

The phone rang again. She ran to answer it. "Aunt Zelena, are you calling me?"

After a high-pitched giggle, a child-like voice chanted in a sing-song rhythm:

"Oh, bad Karen,

Oh, don't you cry for me.

I'll lock you in and tie you up.

You never will be free."

The line went dead.

# Chapter Nine

"Relax, Miss Benoit - Karen - I can't leave my desk, but would you like me to send someone up?" Lou, on duty, reacted to Karen's frenzied call with his usual aplomb.

"I'm coming right down! I don't trust anyone around here. Just be there, will you?"

"I'll be here." Five minutes later Karen rushed up to the lobby desk. "Did you find out who made that call?"

"I told you nothing came through here. The board's been quiet for the last half hour. Everyone's in the Big Easy."

"It was a threatening call! It had to come through here!"

"Unless it was room-to-room."

"It was a child. I'd like to know who is staying here with children."

"No kids here since Christmas. Disney World's a bigger draw."

"What about the little girl I saw on the balcony and those kids I saw running around in the lobby?"

"There was a birthday party earlier, but it was over by the time I got here."

"The person on the phone called me by my first name."

"Sounds like a prank - you know, do you keep Sir Walter Raleigh in cans?"

"Not this call. What about someone at the wedding?"

"What wedding?"

"Oh, come on, Lou, the one that was in the dining room. Is it over?" She looked around the lobby. "I don't see any guests; it must have broken up early."

Lou looked confused. "There was no wedding here. I told you, it was a birthday party."

"Is this some kind of conspiracy? Is everyone in this place trying to make me think I'm nuts? *There was a wedding in that room!*"

She threw open the door to the dining room and stalked into an almost empty room. A few startled diners looked up. Remnants of cowboy and clown wrapping paper littered the floor and a few helium balloons clung to the ceiling. There were no white flowers as she had seen before, no candles, even the piano was gone.

She ran back to Lou at the desk. "Alright, what's going on? I tell you I saw a wedding taking place in there this morning!"

"I don't know, Karen. Maybe you better lie down for a while. Could be too much celebration last night?" he added hopefully.

She glared at him. "You disappoint me. I thought you were different from everyone here, turns out you're part of the same mold. I'm going for a walk."

Ignoring curious stares, Karen exited the hotel without a backward look.

People around here could be living two hundred years ago, she fumed as she retraced her way to town. Obviously she was no longer welcome at her aunt's, so if she came across anything reasonable she'd consider it. The St. Francis was impossible - in spite of a very agreeable night clerk.

She was in town before she realized it. Strolling the main street, she searched for a motel but saw only the usual hodge-podge of small-town stores and diners. At the end of the business district, she came upon a few clapboard houses contrasting drastically with the plantation homes on Loop Road. She walked a short distance before she came to a small white bungalow with the sign 'Bed and Breakfast' tacked to the front door. A white picket fence surrounded the house, locking in a neat green lawn fringed with tulips and ranunculus.

Suddenly she heard her name and looked around for the caller, but the street was deserted. "Karen!" The cry came again, this time from the house directly in front of her. A curtain in one of the windows moved slightly as if someone was looking out, and the screen door flew open. A little girl darted out of the house and down the walkway shouting, "Wait up!" as she shot past Karen, corn-row braids sticking out behind her skinny, dark neck.

Karen wondered what the house was like inside. As she walked toward it, a glitter on the lawn caught her eye. The little girl's running feet must have trampled down the grass, exposing a small gold bracelet, which Karen picked up, planning to give it to whoever opened the door.

When she knocked on the screen door, she was surprised at the sudden chill in the air. A child's silhouette shadowed the screen. Feeling foolish, Karen considered leaving the bracelet and going back to the hotel without asking about the room, but the door was opened before she could make a quick get-away. A high, childish voice called out, "Can I help you?"

Peering up at Karen was a little girl who looked to be about six years old. Soulful, dark eyes stared out of a face pitifully disfigured by harsh scars and puffy skin discolorations. A veil of thick, black hair concealed half the child's face. A shriveled hand crosshatched with red scars and welts protruded from her long-sleeved smock.

"Do you want something?" the child repeated.

Karen hoped her shock wasn't apparent. "Your friend dropped this when she left your house." She held out the small, gold chain.

"That's mine," the girl said, taking the bracelet. "I lost it playing tag."

Before she could stop herself, Karen blurted out the very words she had decided against. "I'm looking for a place to stay. Is your mother home?"

"Come in, my name's Anna" the little girl said, walking back into a dark room bulging with heavy, old-fashioned furniture. It took a moment for Karen to adjust to the darkness before shapeless bulks assumed identity. An over-sized, mahogany secretary stood against the wall, dwarfing other furniture. Faded rose-print covers on a pair of matching, stuffed chairs did nothing to cheer the room. Hand-cro-cheted doilies covered everything. On the mantle, a glass dome trapped a Monarch butterfly posed to take flight. A Life magazine, long out of print, lay open on a coffee table. Karen flipped to the cover exposing the date: February 21, 1997, almost a collectible - and a coincidence. February 21 was today's date.

"I thought you might like some lemonade. Mommy lets me make it when we have visitors." Little Anna placed two glasses and a plate of cookies on the coffee table.

"Lemonade and cookies," Karen murmured. "Like a page out of the past."

"Mommy just finished baking. I'll show you the room that's for rent. You can bring your lemonade if you want."

Karen followed Anna down a narrow hallway, amazed at the little girl's self-confidence. Most children with her appearance would shyly hide in their room, yet Anna seemed poised and sure of herself.

They entered a tiny room that imparted an aura of faded Victorian secrets. Karen could smell lavender. "Your mother likes flowers," she said, noting the large cabbage rose wallpaper which overwhelmed the room's delicate white cane bedroom furniture.

"Yes, ma'am. This is the room for rent. Do you like it?"

"Very nice," Karen said, thinking not a bad place to spend the next three days.

Anna walked back down the hall to a dining room, Karen following. A walnut table, six chairs and an enormous sideboard set with silver candlesticks and an ornate tea service crowded the tiny room. Instead of the busy, flowered wallpaper in the other rooms, Victorian horse-drawn carriages promenaded the walls. "Mommy makes me be careful around this old stuff," Anna said, indicating a china cabinet crammed with cheap knickknacks midst china and crystal.

They entered a large kitchen which was in sunny contrast to the rest of the house and impeccably neat - not the chaotic mess from an afternoon of baking.

"Your mother must be a good housekeeper," Karen said.

Anna took a ribbon from her dress pocket and tied back her bushy hair, making it easier for the bright sunlight to illuminate her ravaged face. Unbelievable that a mother would let her daughter go through life so disfigured, Karen thought, wondering the cause of the scars.

The little girl sat at a table covered with a yellow oilcloth. "You can sit if you want. I would have given you strawberry ice cream, but Daddy didn't take me to the ice cream parlor today." She left the room, returning immediately with the plate of cookies. "We can have pecan cookies instead. I love mama's cookies, but I hate shelling the dumb pecans."

"I remember picking pecans when I was your age."

"Mama always makes *me* pick them."

"I haven't seen your mother yet."

"She's here. Probably busy. You know how moms are."

"No, I never knew my mother - or my father. You're lucky to have someone make cookies for you."

Anna stared at Karen. "I know it."

"I don't know why I said that, you can't be interested in other people's problems-" Karen stopped, dismayed at what she had implied.

"It's okay. You didn't say anything wrong."

Embarrassed, Karen stumbled on, "I don't really miss my parents, since, as I said, I never knew them, but I do miss having someone love me instead of being raised by a lot of families who never had time for me."

Anna regarded Karen with a composure unnatural for one so young. "That's too bad. Why didn't you have a mother and father?"

"Forget I said that. It's not your concern."

"Sometimes it's good to talk about sad things." She removed her bracelet and handed it to Karen. "Here. You can wear this while you're here. It means we're friends."

Not wishing to hurt the child's feelings, Karen took the bracelet. "That's very nice of you, I'll be careful with it." She looked at her watch. "It's getting late. I've got some errands to do. Please ask your mother to call me. Will you be all right till she gets back?"

"Sure."

Karen wrote her name and the hotel on a piece of paper. "I don't know the number of the St. Francis, but she'll be able to find it."

"Yes, ma'am. I've been there."

"Thank you for letting me wear your bracelet, Anna."

"You're welcome, Karen. You can give it back to me before you go home."

"Of course." Karen hesitated, not sure of how to end this strange conversation, then walked out into the bright sunlight. After a moment she turned and spoke through the screen door. "Your mother can leave a message at the hotel, okay?

"Yes'm," Anna's voice floated from the dark recesses of the house.

Out of the corner of her eye, Karen saw a curtain in one of the windows fall into place, as if someone had been watching.

# Chapter Ten

On her way back to the hotel, Karen came to a school and saw several children playing on swings and slides in the front yard. Perhaps the girl on the balcony was enrolled here. No sign to indicate the name of the school.

She was about to enter the building to see if she could get information that no one else was willing to give, when she saw a little girl standing by herself near the entrance. She looked familiar and very lonely. In fact she was crying. Her frail body shook as silent tears streamed down her cheeks. Karen looked around to see if anyone would come to the rescue of the forlorn little girl, but everybody was too busy swinging and jumping rope; there were no teachers in sight. Not a very well monitored playground, she mused. When she turned back the child was gone.

Curious, she entered the school. The boys and girls she passed in the hallway were uniformly dressed and somber in mood as opposed to the laughing children in the schoolyard.

A sign over one of the doors read 'Office.' Karen entered the room and a slight, bony woman behind the counter looked up from a ledger.

"I'm Mrs. Fielding. May I help you?" she asked in the slow, Southern drawl Karen had become accustomed to.

"I'm visiting Bayou Vieux for a few days and was curious about a little girl who might go to this school," Karen said cautiously, hoping the woman wouldn't take her for a pedophile.

"Saint Mary's is an orphanage -"

Karen's hands trembled as she groped for the nearest chair and abruptly sat down. An orphanage! Was this where she began what life she could remember?

"Can I get you a glass of water? You don't look well." The small woman was bending over her.

"I'm fine. I was walking in the hot sun and got dizzy." The woman waited. "I might have stayed here once. Karen Benoit? Do you have any records on me? Around fifteen years ago?"

"We're not allowed to give information without a court order."

"I have identification." She displayed her driver's license. "See? I have no recollection of my past, and I think I might have lived here."

"I told you; we don't give out information on our children."

"But this is about me! I only have a few days here, then I go back to California. I'd just like to know if I ever lived here. Can't you see if my name is in your files?"

The woman hesitated. "I don't suppose it could hurt. The search might take a few minutes. Fifteen years is a long time." She called to someone in the next room. "Jennifer? Would you answer the phone and take any messages while I'm gone?"

A uniformed teenager came into the front office and stood sullenly behind the counter. "Yes'm."

After Mrs. Fielding went into the back room, Karen studied the brooding girl, wondering if *she* had been as uncommunicative at that age. The first six or seven years were a blank. She had no recollection of learning to read or losing her first tooth or visiting Santa Claus, none of the usual childhood memories. Nothing until she was eight or nine years old and discovered how cruel the world could be to a shy, frightened child. She vaguely remembered being hustled out of a dark, shadowy house and trying to explain bruises to a stern nurse. After that, memories of depressing foster homes tumbled about in her mind until the day she found freedom in a sunny California climate.

The woman returned with a thin manila folder. "It took less time than I expected." Karen's heart jumped at the sight of the papers. "May I read it?"

"Sorry, that goes beyond my executive powers. I'll answer one or two questions, then I must get back to work." She turned to the unhappy teenager, "Thank you, Jennifer, you may go now. We won't need you any more today."

"Yes, Mrs. Fielding." A ghost of a grin flitted across the girl's face as she left the room.

"Jennifer is dependable, though moody. We're trying to bring her out of her shell."

Fat chance in this mausoleum, Karen thought grimly. "If I can't read the records, can you tell me anything of my parents?"

"All I can tell you is that you were brought in by your aunt, a Mrs. Zelena D'Aquin of Bayou Vieux. The date of admission was June 16, 1998."

"Not *Mr.* D'Aquin, too?

"Your aunt was alone when she admitted you. You remained at Saint Mary's until the year 2000, when you went to live with foster parents in Baton Rouge. That's all the information we have in our files because then you were transferred to state records in Baton Rouge."

"Are you sure that's all you can tell me?"

The administrator scanned the file, hesitated, then looked up. "I really shouldn't."

"It's my life, Mrs. Fielding. I need to know if there's anything in my background that might cause problems today."

The woman studied the files, paused, then said: "According to the records, you were in a catatonic state when you were brought here and remained secretive and aloof until your departure two years later."

"Catatonic! That would explain a lot. Were you here then?"

"I've only been here for five years. I would have remembered if a child was admitted in that condition."

"Is there anyone who might have worked here then?"

"Perhaps Nurse Lehman, but she's on vacation. The church likes to move us around so the children won't grow too dependent upon us. You can understand that."

She couldn't, but didn't want to make an issue of it. "Does the nurse live in town?"

"I'm sorry, I'm not allowed to-"

"Will you call and see if she's home? It's very important, Mrs. Fielding."

The woman sighed. "I'll make the call from my office. I can't promise anything."

"You've been very helpful!"

Karen sat quietly, trying to see herself as a silent, friendless six-year-old. Nowhere in her memory did that little girl exist.

Mrs. Fielding returned in less than five minutes. "You're in luck. Gloria Lehman is willing to see you. She's somewhat vague these days, but enjoys company. Here's her address. She's leaving tomorrow for her sister's home in Mississippi."

"Is 1388 Magnolia nearby?"

"Three blocks away. Turn to your right when you leave Saint Mary's. Go three blocks and turn right on Magnolia. There's an ice cream parlor on the corner."

"Thank you, Mrs. Fielding. The kids outside look like they're having a good time on the swings and slides."

Mrs. Fielding looked puzzled. "There are no swings or slides at Saint Mary's. They were removed years ago. Too many accidents."

Outside Karen saw nothing but concrete surrounding scrubby patches of lawn. Just like the wedding, the playground didn't exist.

Pictures of cats dominated the small, cluttered cottage belonging to Nurse Lehman of Saint Mary's Orphanage. Two half-packed suitcases spilled open in the middle of the living room, providing sleeping quarters for two Siamese cats. Other felines prowled the house, occasionally lashing out at each other.

"Who can remember?" the elderly nurse muttered in response to Karen's question. "All those kids."

"I was quiet, maybe cried at night -"

"Who doesn't?" Nurse Lehman picked up a fat, black cat and stroked it. "I'm lucky to get three hours sleep. I can't *wait* to get to my sister's. Never married. Not a kid in the house."

"Fifteen years ago? You must remember *something* about me."

"That's a long time, I can't remember yesterday. You got any idea how many kids fit that description?" She thought a moment. "Wait a sec, a kid was brought in after a fire, never said a thing for months. Was that you?" She squinted at Karen. "Cat got your tongue?" she cackled, kissing the fat cat. "Were you in a fire?"

"I don't know, sometimes I dream about fire -"

The nurse picked up a bag of cat food and began to fill five bowls. "If I don't do this my babies might not get fed. Kid that watches the house doesn't do anything but play the computer." She paused. "Could have been you, names mean nothing. Call next week when I get back. Maybe it'll come back to me."

Clues were mounting but nothing made sense.

*Why couldn't she remember?*

Today Karen had learned that she was a silent, sullen child who may or may not have been involved in a fire, and someone in this town wanted to drive her crazy. What a day.

She saw the ice cream parlor the administrator had described and was about to turn left when suddenly vertigo overpowered her so strongly that she had to cling to a signpost to avoid collapsing. Through a haze, Karen saw a man standing outside the entrance to the ice cream parlor holding the hand of a little blonde-haired girl who looked to be the same, lonely child Karen had seen at St. Mary's. Couldn't be, this child was smaller. Besides, this was obviously a father taking his little daughter in for an ice cream cone - no sad little orphan.

By the time Karen decided her brain was working overtime, the dizziness had vanished, as had the man and his daughter. What she was left with was a strong desire for a strawberry ice cream cone. There was nothing to do but go into 'Arty's Ice Cream Parlor' and satisfy her craving.

The store was deserted except for the man and his daughter seated at the back of the store. Strange, she could have sworn the child had been blonde, but this little girl had long, brunette curls hanging down her back.

"Can I help you, ma'am?"

She snapped out of her revelry and focused on the skinny teenager standing before her enveloped in a huge, chocolate smeared apron. "Are you all right, ma'am?"

Ma'am, always ma'am - what was she, a dowager?

"Where are the booths?"

"Ma'am?"

"There used to be booths in here." She remembered a different look to this sweetshop with the round, marble-topped tables.

"Not since *I* been working here, ma'am."

"How long has that been?"

"Three months."

"It was called 'Jimmy's'.

"Yes, ma'am, that's my name. How'd you know?"

"No, I mean this place. 'Jimmy's'. I remember eating strawberry ice cream cones at 'Jimmy's."

"This is Arty's, ma'am. Would you like the Strawberry Macaroon or the Strawberry Ripple?

"You mean you don't sell just plain strawberry ice cream?"

"Nobody wants the plain stuff, ma'am. They want special stuff like -"

"- Strawberry Ripple. Gotcha. So give me a double scoop of Strawberry Ripple and chocolate."

"What kind of chocolate, ma'am?"

"Does it have to have a name?"

"Chocolate Mousse is good. Chocolate Ripple, Chocolate -"

"A scoop of Strawberry Ripple and a scoop of Chocolate Ripple."

"Waffle or sugar cone?"

The craving was gone. At that point Karen didn't care if she ate a plate of licorice flavored mashed potatoes. She looked around and wondered why she had entered this pink and white confectionary in the first place. The man and his daughter were gone, probably slipped out a back exit. Frowning, Jimmy repeated his earth-shattering question.

"Sugar will be fine," she said flatly.

He filled the cone from the ice cream bin and came back to her. "Here you go, ma'am. That'll be seven dollars."

"Did you say *seven* dollars?"

"Yes, ma'am." He turned surly. "Is that a problem?"

She studied the minuscule balls of ice cream, already melting - her hands sticky as they grasped the gummy cone.

"Napkins?"

"In the container on the counter, ma'am."

"If you call me 'ma'am' one more time I'll pummel you with liquid ice cream!"

Jimmy glanced nervously behind Karen, probably wondering if he could make it to the open door before she attacked him with a tub of strawberry ice cream. "You want me to get you a napkin, m-?" He swallowed the 'ma'am' before it came out.

"For seven dollars you should give me the whole container!"

Pleased with the day's discoveries, although mystified by certain events, Karen walked back to the hotel happier than when she had left. She had found the orphanage she had lived in, learned why she had no memory and the possible cause of her nightmares involving fires, and had a potential replacement for the unpleasant hotel. She fingered the bracelet Anna had given her. And made a new friend, however young.

On impulse she entered the cemetery, even though the sun had begun to slip behind a row of flowering dogwoods. She walked fast, not anxious to stumble around antique graves after dark, yet fascinated by the confusion of color and trinkets surrounding each headstone. 'Rida Beauregard, 1920 - 1980' was the only identification on the first tomb she came to, yet a book could be written about the memorabilia around it. A picture of a hefty young woman holding two dimpled babies was framed in a cheap, plastic setting and bore the statement 'We love you, Mama'. Tiny American and French flags bordered the grave; a ball of twisted red yarn was anchored to the ground by a splintered knitting needle; a square glass ashtray inscribed 'souvenir of Niagara Falls' was next to the yarn. Someone had placed two pennies in the ashtray.

A whiskey jug stood in the middle of the next marker with two glasses surrounding the words: 'He died happy.'

A penny arcade atmosphere assaulted this French-Catholic section of the beloved buried. Candy wrappers and paper plates indicated hungry mourners.

Further ahead, in an area separated by low-lying hedges, was the Protestant section of the cemetery decorated with a few formal flower arrangements, none of the frivolity of the Catholic section, but most of the time the graves were bare.

Rows of seven-foot long biers stacked one upon the other, sometimes as high as ten feet tall, lined cemetery walls which concealed grinning skulls and gleaming bones. Here lay the less prosperous of Bayou Vieux; the rich were entombed in above-ground crypts, adorned with marble statues and polished urns. No high-rise burials for them.

Walking along the path, Karen noticed the dates on the grave stones were older. Occasionally a potted plant graced a stone, but more often they were bare. One unadorned tomb read: 'Jacques Guilliem, notre fils qui a mort pour la Confederacy. Nee 1843 - mort 1863.' She picked a buttercup from the moist ground around the grave and placed it on the grave. "Sleep well, Jacques," she said, "*someone* remembers you."

The setting sun cast long shadows, and Karen had almost reached the end of the park when she saw a marble statue of a little girl atop a small, raised bier. There was a sweet sadness to the carved features; Karen was touched by the eloquent remembrance of one who had lived so briefly. She could read the engraved first name, 'Joanna', but weeds obscured the remaining letters.

Shivering in the cool twilight breeze which penetrated her thin jacket, Karen walked quickly out of the park. When she returned to the hotel there were still no messages.

# Chapter Eleven

$\mathcal{B}$ack in her room, Karen used her cell phone to call the D'Aquin's residence, and was pleasantly surprised to hear her uncle's voice. "This is Karen Benoit," she said bluntly, ready for any and all opposition.

"Is there something I can do for you?"

"Yes, you may tell my aunt I want to speak to her." She waited. "Did you hear me, Mr. D'Aquin? I'm getting tired of my aunt's refusal to see me, and I would appreciate it if you would."

"You're persistent, Miss Benoit, but as I said before, my wife is ill and not up to having visitors."

"What about your guests?"

"What about them?"

"I'm not naive, Mr. D'Aquin. Since there are *no* guests, I think you owe me an explanation of why you lied to me."

"When we first spoke, guests were expected, but since then they have changed their minds about arrival dates. We have tried to make you as comfortable as possible. I hope you remember to charge your hotel bills to me. I'm not sure what more I can do."

"You can let me speak to my aunt."

"When my wife is better she will meet with you."

"I'm leaving Wednesday, whether or not this meeting takes place. Perhaps *you* could take the time to answer a few questions."

"I will not go behind my wife's back, Miss Benoit," he said quietly, and hung up.

After a purposefully frigid shower, Karen's fury went down a few notches.

The emerald-green sweater Corky had insisted she borrow looked good on her, which wasn't a bad thing considering she might run into Bo after dinner.

Tonight's jambalaya wasn't as spicy as yesterday's, unless her taste buds had grown accustomed to Cajun delicacies.

"Eat that stuff late at night and you'll be dreaming about more than snakes." Bo's hand on her shoulder sent a slight charge through her body.

"Do you always sneak up on people like that?"

"Just good-looking blondes." He straddled a chair. "And you look terrific in green."

Maybe Corky wasn't so dumb after all. "There never seems to be anyone in the dining room. Don't people like to eat around here?"

"Probably all in New Orleans watching parades."

"How's the studying coming?"

"Rough, but necessary. I've seen too many ODs from pollywog poultices and goofer dust when a good modern drug could work in minutes. The lack of facts is appalling down here, although I won't discount *all* herbal remedies."

"Or hot milk."

He grinned. "Mother's advice."

"Are you going to practice here when you get settled?"

"Yes, ma'am. I be born, raised and pro'bly dig my grave in Bayou Vieux. And dat be de truth, jeune fille."

She frowned. "Why are you talking like that?"

"Us Cajuns, we no parler bon talk, mam'zelle. We be née comme dat."

"You sound like there's something wrong with being Cajun."

"Just the opposite. We're a superior race of people. I just wanted you to know I'm a swamp rat before you find out from somebody else."

"Is that so important?"

"It is to grand old Creole families like the D'Aquins."

"Well, you're talking to a Benoit so there's no need to act huffy."

"Sorry. Guess I'm not the standup comic I thought I was."

She shifted to less volatile grounds. "You must study under a sun lamp, you're so tan." She was beginning to sound like Corky.

"I study in the dead of night when the rest of the world fights off quicksand and snakes."

"Still with the jokes."

"Sorry. I could use a good sensitivity class."

"You didn't answer my question. Or is that none of my business?"

"How come it's all about me?"

She sighed. "I wanted to hear about somebody else for a change." She stood up.

"Hadn't you better get back to work?"

He pulled her back down. "We keep treading on each other's toes. Why do you keep getting mad? I want to talk about *you*. You're interesting and I like you."

"For a lab rat."

"There you go again. Truce?"

He held out his hand. She paused, then put her hand in his, briefly enjoying the touch. Just as quickly she pulled away, reminding herself that nothing must interfere with the reason she was here.

Bo's smile faded. "Buddies again? To answer your question I spend my days hauling shrimp when I'm not studying brain waves. Good source of Vitamin D."

"If you were on a boat today it must have been pretty rough from that tornado."

"What tornado?"

"The one that blasted open my balcony doors. I thought the ceiling was going to cave in."

He frowned. "I'd say today was one of the mildest February days on record. Not a breeze the whole day."

"What are you talking about? My room was a mess. Clothes whipped about like a whirlwind."

"What time was this?"

"Around lunch. Just before I got that damn phone call."

"Obscene?"

"Depends on your definition of the word. Forget it, it wasn't that bad. Just a prankster dialing from somewhere in the hotel. Sounded like a child. Lucius claimed the call didn't go through the switchboard."

"What'd the person say?"

Karen repeated the message.

"Not to be judgmental, but it sounds like a chapter on hallucinations."

Instantly she was on her feet. "Try *paranoid* hallucinations!! I did *not* imagine the call - or the wind - or what happened on the stairs the other day!"

"I've upset you again. I'm sorry, I seem to be spending most of my time apologizing to you."

"That's not true. I'm not always this jumpy, it's just that Bayou Vieux-"

"– is a creepy old town, I know, I know. I guess I'm not the most diplomatic guy in town."

"You could try a little harder to be more tactful."

"I promise." He looked at his watch. "Oh, God, Lou's gonna be climbing the walls. We'll talk later, okay?"

"If I'm not too busy," Karen said coolly, remembering her resolution not to get involved.

Lou looked up as they entered the lobby. "I keep forgetting I'm on Southern time here. 9:00 is really 9:30, right, Bo?"

"Sorry. Hope I didn't make you late for anything."

"Just a hot party in the Quarter, but they usually don't get started till midnight. Have a good one, guys," he said, hurrying out the door.

"Nice guy," Bo glanced through the ledger. "Are you going to your room now?"

"No place else to go. I still haven't heard from my aunt."

"She'll call. I'm here if you need me. Let me know if anything happens."

"Like ghosts rattling chains in my room?"

"If you get another nightmare, write it down, okay?"

"I'm not likely to forget it."

"I didn't want to say anything last night when you were so upset, but folks around here have odd beliefs –"

"Like?"

"Another thing about snake dreams is someone's out to get you."

"Wow, you're going to fit right in when you hang up your shingle. Is this the same medical genius who's going to free the world from psycho-babble?"

"Why are you getting angry again?"

"I'm not a case study. Thanks for the company but I really don't need it."

She marched to the elevator without giving Bo a chance to splutter an answer. Just before the doors closed she saw Tank scurrying around the corner, probably carrying a fistful of dead spiders. He and Bo were two of a kind, no doubt getting ready to howl at the moon.

That night Karen awoke with her breath coming in short gasps.

The nightmare had returned.

A full moon washed the room with stark intensity while a violent wind blasted open the balcony doors, furiously flipping through pages of the book by her nightstand. Her robe slid to the floor in a crumpled heap.

An unseen presence had entered the room.

She trembled as frigid air engulfed her, turning hands and feet to ice. She heard someone - or some*thing* - whispering, then felt her cheek stroked as lightly as butterfly wings brush flowers.

Nightmare or real?

She couldn't tell.

She switched on the nightlight but saw nothing unusual. She reached for the paper and pencil placed on the nightstand three hours earlier, her hand shaking too much to produce anything but a childish scrawl: 'The world is on fire and I cannot escape. I am a child running for my life. As I run, a hand reaches out and clasps my shoulder; the hand becomes the jaws of a snake.' The coldness diminished as she continued to write her dream - and at Bo's request - her feelings.

The next day would be Sunday, the party Tuesday, then good old boring Santa Monica on Wednesday. No more frightening dreams, eerie bayous, gloomy mansions or elusive relatives.

And no more Bo.

A pity, but life never had been overly generous.

# Chapter Twelve

A shrill, persistent phone woke Karen the next day. "Hello?" she mumbled, half asleep. She shook her head trying to unscramble the blur of words leaping over the wire. "Who is this? I can't understand what you're saying."

The whispering continued.

She sprang out of bed. "Mrs. D'Aquin? .... Aunt Zelena, of course Seven tonight. Yes, I'll be there, I'm looking forward to seeing you...yes...goodbye."

So the big event was finally taking place. What to wear? No choice, she hadn't brought that much. Could she wait till seven? She'd go crazy sitting in this room, staring at the four walls. She looked at her watch, astonished. One o'clock. But plenty of time for a stroll to town which might take her mind off the much anticipated conference.

Half an hour later, she stepped into the hall and felt something crunch beneath her shoe. She looked down at a small, leather pouch. Hall shadows made it difficult to see anything inside the bag so she took it back to her room and dumped out the contents on the coffee table. What looked like dust was a blend of colored powders and dry leaves which gave off an odd, acrid odor.

The "leaf" turned out to be snake skin; the red and yellow powder was a mystery.

She poured the repulsive concoction back into the bag and dropped it into her purse, planning to tell Tank not to waste his time with any more 'charms' but the rambunctious child was nowhere in sight when she entered the lobby.

Telemaque looked up from his cards as she approached the desk. "Good morning," she said, sounding more cheerful than she felt. "Looks like another nice day."

"No, Miz Benoit, be rain soon."

"Now why do you say that? There're no clouds."

"Old Falfi not dead yet. She go, dey be plenty rain, you see."

She sighed. More nonsense. "And who is Falfi if I'm not too nosey?"

"She be oldest woman in village. She so old her mama be sold in slave market in Congo Square. Old Falfi dying now, can't last much longer."

"I'm sorry to hear that, but what's that got to do with rain?"

"Cajuns say dey be storm after death of old woman."

"And you believe that?"

"It not be wrong yet, Miz Benoit."

Useless to reason with doggedness. "Have you seen Tank?"

"Tank, he not be in yet."

"He must have left that thing by my door last night. I saw him run through the lobby."

"What thing, Miz Benoit?"

She withdrew the little pouch from her purse and placed it on the counter. At the sight of the strange object Telemaque's eyes grew bright with horror. He crossed himself rapidly three times.

"What's the matter? Why are you looking like that?"

"Where you get dis, Miz Benoit?"

"It was outside my door. Tank said something about giving me cemetery dirt to ward off ghosts. I told him ghosts didn't exist. Poor kid, he even scares himself."

Telemaque was hypnotized by the bag. "Tank never put dat in front of you door. Tank, he be good boy. Dat be *bad* gris-gris. Powerful voodoo. When goofer dust mix with snake skin and red ash, it drive person fou-de-tete. Tank never give you dat bad gris-gris."

"What is *wrong* with everyone? Now you're telling me someone is trying to drive me crazy? Is that what fou-de-tete means?"

"That be so if someone give you gris-gris," Telemaque insisted solemnly.

"That's ridiculous! I never heard of Bayou Vieux until three weeks ago. Why should anyone be after me? Unless -" Karen was silent a moment, unwilling to express her growing doubts.

"You be careful, Miz Benoit, put holy picture on you door tonight. Maybe Jesus or Mother Mary, comprendez? Keep away evil."

At that point Lucius fairly flew through the revolving doors and crashed exhausted at the counter.

"Okay Telemaque, you can go now." Lucius stashed his backpack under the counter. "Sorry I'm late, traffic was a bitch."

"That's all right, Lou. Me, I be telling Miz Benoit, she gotta be careful in Bayou Vieux. They's all kinda bad things 'round here."

"Hey, don't be trying to scare the lovely lady off. You know that's all bull shit."

"You ain't be here long enough to know facts, man," Telemaque muttered as he shuffled off toward the back door.

Karen hated to see the old man looking so despondent - especially since she was the cause. "I'll be careful, Telemaque, I promise!" she called after him.

He turned and she saw the anxiety in his eyes "Please, Miz Benoit, you take care. Dis hotel not good for you."

"Nothing's going to happen to me."

"Yes'um." He shrugged and left the room.

Lou laughed. "The old guy's full of it like everyone else around here. Don't give up on us, Karen. We're not all in the Dark Ages."

"Maybe not, but I'm still leaving as soon as I find something in town."

"Something I said?"

"No way. You're probably the only normal person I've met in this weird place. If you ever get to Santa Monica, look me up. We've got sunshine, beaches - and no gris- gris!"

Every newcomer must be exposed to the same gibberish, she deliberated as she walked to town. Maybe it's part of some damn advertising campaign: "Visit Bayou Vieux - spookiest town in America!" Or they might be getting ready to shoot a movie. Gloomy bayous and ghostly mansions guarantee a big box office.

Or maybe they *want* to scare visitors away, herself included. So why the invitation? Telemaque was right about the hotel giving off bad vibes. She wondered fleetingly if haunted houses really existed.

She was in the clapboard section of town before she knew it.

So where was the bed and breakfast place? She'd recognized a few buildings, had even passed Arty's and Saint Mary's, where was Anna's house? There was nothing but a dilapidated playhouse under an enormous pecan tree where she though the house should be. Maybe she'd written down the wrong address. Too late she realized she hadn't asked the child's last name. Maybe she *was* going nuts. Or nutti*er*, as Corky would say.

And maybe the child's mother would call, she knew where Karen was staying. Meantime she'd take a quick look at the library, do some research on the haughty Richard D'Aquin and elusive Zelena D'Aquin who kept putting her off.

Five minutes later she was standing in front of the library she had noticed two days earlier, a dismal, stone building. Perhaps her old friends, books, would be more informative than the arrogant townspeople she had encountered thus far. As she passed under the ribbed vaults of the ancient building she decided the library was constructed at the same time as the St. Francis Hotel; they had the same Gothic, medieval look.

The interior was cold and impersonal after bright sunlight; and the scattering of stained glass windows portraying archaic literary figures spread neither joy nor light. As Karen approached the desk, a gnome-like figure peered at her over a book, the tiny woman's eyes distorted by thick glasses anchored firmly to her nose.

"I'm Mrs. Hester. May I help you?" the woman asked in a quivery voice.

"Do you keep old newspapers? About twenty-five years old?"

"Does this concern local news?"

"Yes."

"We have the New Orleans Times-Picayune on file which sometimes contains items about Bayou Vieux."

"Would the papers go back that far?"

"My dear, we have copies dating back to South Carolina's secession. *Southerners* know the value of history," she sniffed, implying the rest of America didn't.

"Where may I find the newspapers?"

"In the stacks," she said, pointing to a room beyond a marble arch. "If you don't find what you're looking for try the room upstairs. The archives in there only go back fifty years."

"I'm sure this will be fine."

"Call me if you need me."

"I don't have the time to look right now, but I'll be back."

"As you wish," Mrs. Hester adjusted her bifocals and went back to the days of Scarlett and Rhett.

# Chapter Thirteen

Promptly at seven o'clock that night Karen was pounding the wolf-knocker on the D'Aquin front door, uneasily anticipating deep-throated growls from the dogs. She knew they were there. Two, she decided. Large and menacing, not the yappy little white dogs of Santa Monica. They would be wild, yet controlled by someone even more commanding than her aunt whom she pictured as frail and boney. Odelia? Yes, Odelia could control large dogs. The door opened and there stood her nemesis in all her glowering glory. What *was* her problem? For whatever reason, the sullen housekeeper most decidedly hated Karen, and they both knew it.

She refused to be intimidated.

"Good evening, Odelia, will you tell my aunt I'm here?"

"Miz D'Aquin, she be sick."

Karen lost her temper.

"This is getting ridiculous! My aunt called me today and asked me specifically to come to dinner at 7 PM. And here I am. Right on time - as usual!"

"And dinner be ready - as usual," Odelia muttered as she wafted back into murky shadows, leaving Karen fuming.

"Are they there?" Karen shouted into the dark regions of Odelia's disappearance. "My aunt and uncle? I insist on seeing them *now*! Do you understand?" She glimpsed a slight movement from the balcony above and her head jerked upward. "Mrs. D'Aquin? Aunt Zelena? Is that you up there? Can you hear me? Are you coming down now? If so, I'm here, waiting for you!"

Karen realized she had gone too far; the shadow was gone. She heard retreating sounds of a dog panting, then silence.

She rushed into the dining room, set for one.

"No!" she shouted "I will not be put off again! This is outrageous! You're playing games with me!" She raged around the room, rattling doorknobs, kicking the walls like a petulant child till fury subsided and she sank, exhausted, into a regal dining room chair adjacent to a buffet crowded with pictures.

Overwhelmed by the unexpected barriers hindering her search for her background, Karen's eyes wandered aimlessly over the barrage of family heritage on walls, tables and counters.

One ivory-framed picture caught her attention. Enormous eyes black as the night surfaced from a face cut from marble, hair like ebony Spanish moss surrounded perfect features. The woman in the frame was ageless. Next to this compelling photograph was a portrait of a little girl, possibly five or six years old - hard to say because of the romanticized style so popular with painters. Cherub, pouty lips, sad, dark eyes showing more sorrow than she needed to see. Thick black hair crimped into ringlets fashionable centuries past. Even this painter of pretty pictures couldn't wipe away the misery in the little girl's face.

"Dinner be served!" Odelia's flat voice broke into Karen's thoughts.

"Who is this child?" Karen asked, not really expecting an answer.

"She be precious little lamb. Mama's little angel. Best child in de world next to little Odette." Odelia's praises continued to overflow into worship-like homilies.

"But who *is* she? Is she the daughter of the D'Aquin's?"

"Don't matter who she be, lady, she be dead."

Karen stiffened. That explained a lot. If this child were the daughter of Zelena and Richard D'Aquin and died at a young age, perhaps the couple never really recovered from the tragedy. Well, that was *their* problem, she'd had enough of the whole irrational family.

She was aware of Odelia standing behind her, no doubt waiting for her to sob with angst. "If you see my aunt or uncle tell them I'm not hungry," she said, bolting for the front door, not caring what Odelia thought of her lack of sympathy.

Just as Karen turned into the driveway of the Saint Francis she glanced up at the old hotel. The three-story building looked like it was cut in half showing the first and third floors ablaze with lights. The third floor floated mysteriously in space as the floor beneath it remained dark and disquieting. She parked the car and entered the hotel through the back entrance.

"Look who's here," Bo said as Karen approached the front desk.

"Still got your nose in the books, I see."

"Always. I rang your room but you were out."

There was a pause, then both blurted out at the same time, "Look, I'm sorry if-"

"I didn't mean to -"

Bo grinned. "Apres vous, ma petite."

"You first."

"I wasn't making fun of you, Cherie. I was concerned. I guess I could have been more diplomatic."

"For sure, garcon."

"You're catching on to our patois. So, how'd it go tonight? Were you at your aunt's?"

"No aunt. How do you say that in Cajun? Not even an uncle this time."

"There's a bright side. The longer your aunt stays in bed the more I get to see you."

"There is no bright side. I have to go back on Wednesday. If I don't find out about my mother by Tuesday, I never will. The whole trip will have been a waste of time."

"Please don't say that, Cherie. At least I got to meet you."

"For what it's worth."

"It was worth a lot to me."

Karen avoided his eyes and tried to look impassive.

He sighed. "So Tuesday's the big day?"

"So the invitation read."

"Anything to do with Mardi Gras? Same day."

"I doubt they'd ask me out here just for that."

"I wish you'd stay longer. I really would like to get to know you better."

"More case studies?"

"You know that's not true."

"Cards have deadlines. I have to get back."

"Then we better make the most of it while you're here. Have you seen the countryside?"

"I stopped at a bayou my first day. It was beautiful - so many swamp birds."

"Egrets and herons. I'll pack a picnic basket, and pick you up at noon to-morrow."

Her eyes widened in indignation. "You're assuming I'll say yes."

"I don't mean to be pushy, but have you anything better to do?"

She laughed ruefully. "Not if my aunt doesn't call."

"If she does then we won't go."

"Then it's a deal."

"Good. I'd love to show you around - and show you off. Wear something easy because I'll take you out in a pirogue, maybe spot an eagle or a few 'gators."

"I'm okay with eagles but forget the 'gators."

"They won't hurt you if you don't hurt them, and I don't think you're the type to argue with one."

A rowdy foursome danced up to the counter. By their costumes they were either pre- or post- parade.

Karen eased away from a leering Joker. "I better let you get back to work."

"See you at noon," Bo called as she started toward the elevator.

Karen hummed as she pressed the third floor button and entered the car, but became increasingly uneasy as the ancient crate creaked toward the second floor. Suddenly it shuddered to a stop and the doors of the elevator started to open. She pushed the third floor button and waited for the tortoise-like crawl to resume. The doors closed but the car stayed where it was. She jabbed the button again. Nothing. She felt a chill inch into the normally hot, stuffy car and looked around for an escape hatch - she would *not* get out on the second floor. Thankfully the old crate was equipped with a phone. She rattled the receiver. "Answer, damn it, Bo," she muttered, and almost giggled with relief when she heard his voice.

"You okay, Karen?"

"I'm stuck on the second floor. The elevator won't go any further."

"Will the doors open?"

"I don't know."

"They should - it was fixed last month. Push the emergency button and when it opens walk down the hall to the stairs. I'll check the elevator when I get off in the morning."

"Bo, I'm not budging! It's pitch black out there."

"These guys are getting rowdy down here; I can't leave the desk There's a light switch left of the elevator as you step out. Turn it on and come down here instead of going to your room. I'll take a break as soon as these jokers go away. Karen? Did you hear what I said?"

"Yeah, okay... I'll be down in a minute."

"Good. Don't worry, I'm right here." He hung up.

After the doors opened, Karen peered into the murky hall - like looking into an inkwell. The doors began to close again. "Oh, no you don't," she muttered and punched the button oven and over until the doors reopened. The elevator light could guide her to the hall switch, but she needed to wedge something between the doors to keep them apart; her purse was too lightweight to stand the pressure if the doors slammed shut. With nothing else to act as doorstop she'd just have to make a dash for it. She groped her way to the switch, frustrated that the light was too dim to see more than a foot in front of her.

Suddenly the elevator doors slid shut and she was left in total darkness. She fumbled along the wall, breaking two fingernails before reaching the switch. Instantly, a dim overhead light pierced the darkness, casting dark shadows in the hollows of nearby doorways. Better than nothing.

Robot-like, she started down the dim hallway, ears ringing from the pressure of her heartbeat. Her skin was clammy as if she had just emerged from a hot spa into the coolness of a mountain breeze. She could barely see the emergency exit at the end of the hall, and hoped her legs would carry her that far.

As she minced along the passageway, clinging to walls, laughter came from a room she was passing. Impossible, the floor was empty. A shrill, child-like giggle grew louder, then softer as if someone were playing hide-and-seek. Karen stood still, sensing a breathing presence on the other side of the door.

"Is someone there?" she asked cautiously, startled by the sound of her own voice. "Is everything all right?"

Silence was the response, as if someone inside was listening.

What if whoever was in the room, a child perhaps, was being held prisoner? The little girl on the balcony? She pounded on the door. "Do you need help?"

Still no reaction. She twisted the copper doorknob, surprised by the heat of the knob. The door swung open, revealing a red glow from the room within. Then, as if possessing a life of its own, the door slammed violently against the wall. At the same time she heard a terrified scream and saw a raging fire leaping around the four walls of the room. A figure engulfed in flames thrashed about blindly, trying to escape the holocaust.

As Karen watched in horror, the blazing shape shambled toward her, screaming unintelligible sounds. At the last moment, before the flaming, outstretched fingers could touch her, Karen backed out of the fiery room and ran toward the exit, covering her ears to shut out the grotesque cries of a person being swallowed alive by fire.

Her last thought before crumpling to the floor was why no one had unlocked the emergency door.

# Chapter Fourteen

Karen woke up screaming, fighting to free herself from imprisoning arms.

"Shh, ma petite, it's all right." Gentle hands brushed damp hair from her face as a voice whispered calming words.

She opened her eyes and saw again the creature bathed in fire stumbling toward her. "NO!" she screamed, whipping her head back and forth to escape the image before her.

"Karen, you're safe! Nothing is happening. It was a dream, yes?"

Her gaze settled on the man bending over her: Bo, once again the rescuer.

"It was *not* a dream! We've got to help that person!" She tried to spring to her feet but had no strength; her legs buckled and she fell to the floor.

Bo eased her to a standing position and led her, protesting, back to bed. "Karen, you're all right. There's nothing to be frightened of. I'm here, nothing can hurt you."

"You're not listening to me! A room is on fire; do you understand? Someone in there is dying! We've got to help!"

This time Karen made it to the door, but Bo caught her before she could escape, gripping her arms as tightly as if she were in a strait jacket.

"There's *no* fire, Karen! You're in your room. I'm with you. You're safe with me! Are you hearing me?"

"The fire's not *here*! On the *second* floor. We've got to put it out!"

"There's no fire anywhere." He stroked her hair until the trembling stopped.

"What are you talking about? I *saw* it!" she hissed.

"No fire."

Her breathing slowed until she no longer felt her heart would burst from her chest.

"When you didn't come down I came to check on you. The door to the second floor was locked. Apparently they keep it locked to avoid vandalism. I unlocked it and found you unconscious on the floor. When I tried to lift you, you began screaming about a fire -"

The rage began again. "You don't believe me!"

"Ma petite, I checked every room with you in my arms, fighting like a tiger all the way. I didn't dare put you down. There're ten rooms on that floor, every one of them pitch-black and colder than a 'gator's belly."

*"Then what did I see?* I wasn't asleep this time! I still have enough sense to tell the difference between a nightmare and reality whether you believe it or not!"

"A reflection from the elevator?"

*"The elevator door was closed!"*

"The hall light was on. You turned it on, remember? The light must have been reflected in a mirror in the room. You were confused, worrying over bad dreams, loss of sleep - you could have imagined it."

"I am *not* confused! I am *not* crazy! Oh, shit!"

"What?"

"The gris-gris! Someone put a gris-gris by my door. That's what made me see the fire! I *am* going crazy!"

"Oh, come on, Karen, you don't believe that nonsense. That's just for superstitious folk like Telemaque or Tank. Bayou folk play that game all day long. Gris-gris, gris-gris, who's got the gris-gris?"

"You took it pretty seriously when you warned me of primitive ways down here."

"I didn't mean to frighten you, I just wanted you to be careful. Cajuns don't like strangers trying to bring them into the computer age. They'd rather work things out their own way."

"But the gris-gris worked, made me see things I wasn't supposed to."

"A nightmare, Karen, that's all you saw."

She was quiet a moment. "I *have* to see that room again!"

"If you feel like going down to check, no one's stopping you, but believe me there was no fire. I wouldn't be standing here arguing if there was." He started for the door. "I'm sorry, I need to be at the desk, but please call me again if you need me."

"All right, all *right!* There was no fire. I heard no screams. I imagined the whole thing!" She paused, hating to beg, then finally blurted out "But can't you stay just a little longer?"

He smiled gently. "Cherie, I'm on duty, I have to go back. If you're afraid to stay alone, come downstairs. We can talk till you feel better."

"You think I'm a coward and a liar."

"I don't think anything of the kind. All nightmares seem real."

She still couldn't let him go. "Does anyone here talk about bad vibes besides me? Guests, staff, anyone?"

"I'm not a regular here so I can't say, but my brother says there're the usual gripes: 'My window won't open, my room is freezing, my room is too hot, the sheets weren't changed today'. His eyes sought hers, needing to convince. "No ghost sightings."

"What about the maids or bellboys like Tank or even Telemaque. Do they say anything?"

"Karen, do you really think this place is haunted?"

"Is it?"

"I don't think any hundred-year-old building in the South would confess to *not* being haunted."

"Goes with the territory, huh?"

"You've seen the pamphlets. I can't speak for those who work here, but you know I don't believe in ghosts - and I'd bet my first year's salary you don't either."

"Right now I won't take that bet."

"You will after you've had a few days to think about it. I've got to get back to the desk."

"You won't go anywhere else, will you?" She hated sounding so dependent.

"I'm here if you need me, Karen." He brushed her forehead with his lips, sending little shocks of pleasure buzzing her body.

"Just make sure those exit doors are unlocked."

"Don't worry, and sleep tight, Cherie," he said as he moved toward the door.

"I'll be fine. And thanks. Without you I'd be climbing walls."

# Chapter Fifteen

*B*ut she hadn't been fine. She had stretched the night out as long as possible, reading until her arms could no longer support a book, then drifted off into a fitful sleep, plagued with formless, frightening visions which left her exhausted, shivering for the relief of daylight.

Three AM and wide awake, Karen was staring at the ceiling as she tried to rationalize the chaos her life had become. A thought, a fragment of a memory, kept slipping in and out of her subconscious as elusive as the wings of a hummingbird. Once more, in her dreams, she saw a fire and a figure stumbling toward her, but this time she hadn't run; she had confronted the thing staggering toward her. "Who are you?" she shouted

"I am Joanna," the dying creature cried.

And then Karen had to know the truth.

She dressed in a sweater, jeans and a jacket, then slipped out into the empty hallway, checking to see if another grisly bag was by her door. Finding none she hurried to the elevator where Bo had scrawled a note: 'Elevator not working, please use stairs.'

The thought of going down those stairs almost turned her back, but driven by her dreams she could *not* turn back. She opened the exit door prepared to break all records for racing down stairs, then almost shouted with joy as the nun staggered into sight, clutching his heart.

"Freaking car's out of order," he wheezed, mopping his brow with his habit.

"I know," she murmured sympathetically. "That's an awful climb."

"Tell me about it. Get your ass up here, Dolly!" he yelled over his shoulder.

Puffing and miserable, Dolly heaved herself up the last step. "Shut up, creep!" she growled as they limped off together down the hall and out of sight.

Cheered by the thought of other earthly bodies inhabiting the hotel, Karen sprinted down the rest of the stairs, unhampered by further attacks.

She sneaked out the back entrance knowing Bo would try to stop her if he saw her going out into the night. He hadn't believed her story about the fire and why should he? There *wasn't* a fire, thank God - but then what had she seen? Was her mind playing tricks or was it something more sinister?

By the time she reached the cemetery the faint mist had become a rolling fog. An ancient street lamp, the kind torn down and replaced by sleek, metallic monsters, cast a gloomy light on the heavy, wrought-iron gates as she pushed them open. Elongated shadows played leapfrog on the path before her, and it took a moment to realize the lumpy, misshapen objects looming in front of her were merely benches in daylight hours. She reached the Catholic section and tried to remember which direction she had taken on Saturday.

Then she saw it.

The drifting fog shifted enough to expose, one aisle over, the statue of a little girl atop a monument. Karen ran past the other graves, heedless of disrespect for the dead, then stepped over the low hedge separating Catholics and Protestants. There, in a night almost too dark to see, her fingers traced the inscription beneath the child's figure. She already knew the first name, but couldn't make out the last. She fumbled in her jacket pocket for matches left over from her smoking days, struck a few limp ones until she was rewarded by a small flare which briefly illuminated the words 'Joanna D'Aquin, Born November 22, 1992, died February 23, 1998. The Gift of Laughter."

February 23 was two days away.

Karen gazed at the small figure until the match burned her fingers. This was her cousin, born only two months before her. Karen felt a sudden sadness at never having known this child with 'the gift of laughter'. Once more she heard herself shouting in her dream, "Who are you?" and the far-off answer, "Joanna." Ivy had obscured the full inscription two days ago but someone had recently pulled the weeds so that both names were now evident. She looked around at the surrounding graves. Only Joanna's was spotless.

Had Odelia mentioned Zelena's daughter's first name? No, she had said the little girl in the picture was dead, that's all. Perhaps the child in this grave was *not* the daughter of Zelena and Richard. D'Aquin was a common French name - there were probably dozens of D'Aquins in and around Bayou Vieux. But whoever she was, Karen knew the Joanna who lay in the grave beneath her feet was the Joanna of her dreams.

She heard a rasping sound at her back and whirled around to see a hugely oversized dog lurching toward her. The fog had lifted slightly and the monster was close enough for Karen to see a glint of fangs. Panicky, she crouched behind the monument, praying she wouldn't be attacked. The beast reached her hiding place, sniffed then turned its massive head directly toward her. She ducked further back into the bushes trying to avoid the vapid stare of the dog's tiny eyes before she realized the animal had no vision.

A rustle of skirts and a low, sharp command caused the dog to halt its bumbling pursuit of Karen.

"Quiet, Zeus! Go away; you're bothering the pretty lady."

The enormous animal flattened his ears and instantly dropped to the ground on his belly. He whimpered as he crawled past his owner, then stood on all fours and trotted off toward the cemetery entrance.

"You don't have to hide any longer. Zeus won't hurt you."

"That's one big dog," Karen murmured, trying to emerge from the bushes with dignity. "What is he?"

"A Great Dane - but he thinks he's a pussy cat. It's good you didn't scream, he's normally gentle, but being blind, he startles easily and is likely to lash out at anything."

"He's well-trained. He obeyed you instantly."

"Oh, yes, he's won many ribbons. I think he was just disturbed to find a stranger at my daughter's grave."

"*Your* daughter? You're Zelena D'Aquin?"

"I am," she replied. The woman tossed back thick, dark hair revealing high cheekbones, sharp, angular features and flashing black eyes. Ageless in the moonlight, wearing a white dress covered by a voluminous white cloak that swept the ground, she was ghost-like in the unearthly surroundings.

"I've waited quite a while to see you - I never dreamed our first meeting would be in a cemetery. I'm Karen Benoit - your niece."

"Ironic, isn't it? I would have preferred the comforts of home, but I have not been well, and my husband has not allowed me to see anyone until he's convinced I've recovered."

"This cool night air might not be good for you."

"It doesn't affect what ails me. Actually the chill is quite refreshing. I often take Zeus out for midnight walks. Sometimes we come here and I communicate with departed friends - purely a one-way conversation, I assure you."

"Of course." The odd locality, the menacing dog and this wraith-like creature who stood before her combined to make Karen think more kindly of rhyming 'moon' and 'June' and addle-brained surfers with sun-streaked hair. At least California had a banality about it that didn't keep her awake nights.

"Your mother is here, you know," her aunt said abruptly, cutting into her thoughts.

"My mother is buried here?" Karen felt cold sweat drench her skin. Answers were popping up so quickly and happening so easily after all these years. "Where? Near us?"

"Up there. On the hill." Her aunt pointed to a large oak tree silhouetted against a bank of drifting clouds made luminous by the moon. Wispy Spanish moss swayed from the oak's branches in perpetual dance.

"Will you take me there?"

"Come by for lunch on Tuesday, and Odelia will prepare a Cajun meal that will rival anything Antoine's has to offer. Then we'll see your mother's grave in the daylight."

"Not till Tuesday? I'm leaving Wednesday. I could come by tomorrow," she said, completely forgetting her picnic with Bo.

"That would not be possible; I have an engagement. We'll have our question and answer period Tuesday morning and leave the frivolities for the evening. Why don't you come by around ten-thirty? My face looks as if it were backed over by a truck if you catch me too early."

"Tuesday morning will be fine," Karen replied, amused by the sheer normality of their conversation.

"Excellent! The estate is lovely in spring. Wild azaleas and dogwood are blooming and the scent of yellow jasmine is intoxicating. We'll have Odelia's famous *courtboullion* and some of her little rice cakes smothered in sugar for dessert if she's in a proper mood. You must excuse my former odd behavior, Karen, but I'm delighted we'll finally have a chance to chat - just the two of us. We won't bother with Richard; we'll see him that night."

"Are you sure it won't be too much for you with the anniversary party that evening?"

"I'm not lifting a finger for either event. And now I must leave you. We're both turning blue. Till Tuesday." She turned to go.

"Aunt Zelena," Karen paused, "I was sorry to hear about your daughter - my cousin. I saw her picture the other night while I was waiting for you. I've been puzzled about certain events so I came here to find answers."

"You're not frightened by cemeteries at night?" Zelena asked curiously. "Then you're not from around here, my dear. Most Bayou Vieux folks would be scared out of their wits."

Karen laughed. "I wasn't scared until Zeus came along. I'm staying close by, so I won't have to run far if spooks chase me."

"You're staying at the St. Francis. Isn't it lucky we're both night wanderers so we could have this little chat?" Zelena caressed her daughter's tomb. "Yes, my daughter is in this cold, dark place. The Good Lord took her away at a very young age." She stroked the smooth marble surface. "We cannot begin to understand how God rules this strange planet called Earth, we must only be patient until the time comes when we will see our loved ones again. Goodbye, Karen, Richard worries if he wakes up and finds me gone, and we'll both turn to stone if we stay much longer."

Zelena hugged Karen and a faint odor of lavender drifted up from the folds of her cloak.

"Goodbye, Aunt Zelena, I'm glad to have finally met you."

"The feeling is mutual." She walked a short distance then called over her shoulder, "Don't forget, Vencus at 10:30 on Tuesday."

"I'll be there."

Karen watched her aunt walk around the grave stones till she was out of sight, and realized that at last she had the terrible yet simple answer to the events of the past few days: her cousin Joanna had died in a fire on the second floor of the St. Francis Hotel and she had picked up impressions of the horrific event. Never a believer in psychic phenomena, she was now ready to accept its existence. She was sorry for the grief her aunt had endured, yet the thought that the woman had turned to her for comfort - perhaps even *needed* her as a replacement for the child she had lost so many years ago - filled Karen with a guilty joy.

She started back to the hotel, thrilled to have finally met her aunt, then stopped, chilled by a sudden thought: if her cousin had died in a fire at the St. Francis, had she, as a child, been witness to that death? Is that why she was brought to the orphanage in a catatonic state? Tuesday she would have all the answers, she felt sure.

# Chapter Sixteen

$\mathcal{I}$t was almost four-thirty in the morning by the time Karen entered the hotel lobby and saw Bo nodding over an immense book. Her state of euphoria from finally meeting her aunt overcame any fatigue she should have had.

She grinned, and slammed her fist on the counter yelling, "Hey you, desk manager! Wake up or I'll report you to the owners!"

Bo leaped to his feet, sending *Diseases of the Mind* crashing to the floor. He grinned when he saw the source of the noisy command. "Good God, Karen, next time blast me with pepper spray!"

"Is this how you study? With your books as a pillow?"

"That or go back to shrimp boats." He rubbed his eyes. "What the hell time is it?"

"Time for you to wake up! We can't have the help sleeping on the job."

'Look at you! You're in a good mood. How was your aunt?"

"How'd you know I saw her?"

"Cajuns are psychic. Where'd you go? It's too early in the morning to be having dates with elderly aunts."

"She's not *that* old. I walked over to the cemetery, and she had the same idea."

"Two crazies prowling graveyards at night could only be related."

"She told me my mother is buried there. I'll find out more on Tuesday. She invited me for lunch."

"I'd say it was about time."

A scowl from Karen told Bo that once again he'd said the wrong thing. "Well, anyway, I'm glad you're feeling better," he finished lamely.

Karen was quiet a moment, then asked shyly, "Is our picnic still on for tomorrow?"

"Of course! The thought of showing you around my bayou kept me going all day."

"I feel like a new person. My aunt was charming, nothing like what I expected."

"It's nice to see you smile. That's a good thing about Cajuns - we're happiest when everyone's happy!"

"Is that some sort of scientific theory?"

"Just good old common sense. The elevator's still not running so I'll walk you to your room."

And after that? They were getting close to each other again, and Karen wanted no further complications at this crucial time of her life. "I can make the trip alone. You're not supposed to leave the desk, remember?"

"It's quiet now. Let's go."

They walked the stairs in silence, Bo's arm lightly around her waist. An icy blast of cold air made her shiver as they passed the second story landing, but Bo pulled her closer and the chill vanished. When they reached the third floor and stopped in front of her door, she fumbled in her purse for the key. As she frantically searched, wishing this intimate moment would be over, Bo turned her toward him and said so softly she could barely hear, "Don't I get a reward?"

Her heart hammered rapidly, he was standing too near. She decided to be flip. "For?"

"Damsels in distress usually reward their rescuers," he murmured in her ear.

"Sorry, no change."

He pulled her to him. "I didn't mean monetarily"

His kiss was as she had imagined, gentle yet hard enough to make her want more. She could feel his heart beating through the rough flannel of his shirt. His lips traveled to her neck and the warm breath on her skin made her dizzy with a need totally foreign to her. She looked up at him, their eyes briefly questioning each other, then she turned away quickly, before she said or did anything she might later regret.

"Not now, Bo. I can't get involved now."

He lifted the hair from the nape of her neck and tenderly kissed her vulnerable flesh. "Oui, ma p'tite, je compris."

"I mean it, Bo, this isn't the right time for me."

"Et demain?" he whispered, gently nibbling her ear lobe.

Karen had an overwhelming desire to find out if Cajuns were as passionate as the French were supposed to be, but knew she could go no further with this man she was becoming so increasingly fond of - at least at the moment. "Tomorrow's another day," she said shakily, and slipped out of his arms. "Thank you for always coming to my aid. I'm not always this needy. I mean -" she blushed at the implication of her words. If Bo caught the double entendre, he didn't show it, "My pleasure, Cherie," he murmured. "See you at noon tomorrow."

Karen shut the door behind her and slipped into her room before he could touch her again.

When she awoke the next morning, the only dreams she could remember were playfully erotic. She lay still a while longer, enjoying the blissful remembrance of Bo's kisses until she glanced at the clock - and instantly sat up with a jolt. Eleven-thirty. She was supposed to be somewhere but where? An image of Bo bending over her flashed in her mind. Their picnic! How could she have forgotten?

She rushed to the bathroom, splashed cold water in her face, and minutes later was struggling into a blouse and jeans. A small chunk of material was missing from the hem of the yellow poppy-print blouse that Corky said turned her into a wild gypsy, and she better bring it to Louisiana if she wanted to have some *real* fun. Karen had brought the blouse to shut Corky up, but now decided it was the right thing to wear today. A glance in the mirror told her she needed a dash more lipstick and a helluva lot more mascara if the blouse was to work its magic The pathetic thing about being a natural blonde was having eyelashes to match, so if she wanted to avoid looking like a corpse she'd better get out the Maybelline. She wrapped her new silk scarf around her neck and fluffed her hair into studied disarray. The creature that stared back at Karen looked a hundred time more vivacious than the bookworm who had limped in from California a few days ago. She could hear Corky saying, '*You go, girl!*'

She entered the lobby expecting to see Telemaque but found instead Lou looking miffed.

"Aren't you early?" she asked the usually laid-back clerk.

He yawned. "Telemaque didn't show. I'm not used to going to work at five in the morning. That's the time I normally go to bed."

"Is he all right?"

"No idea. But someone better take my shift today or they can replace me permanently. I've had it up to here with the Deep South. California calls."

"You'll have plenty of weird plots to take with you. Hollywood loves the bizarre."

"Exactly what I was thinking."

Karen looked around. An elderly couple played backgammon at one of the game tables and several guests read while others talked in low tones. She checked her watch. Twelve-fifteen. She sat on an unoccupied couch and skimmed through a five-year-old Reader's Digest which reminded her of little Anna's outdated Life magazine.

Anna's mother had never called. Odd. Perhaps the child had forgotten to give the message. Conditions in the old hotel seemed to have improved, she was no longer a candidate for electric shock every time she went up and down the stairs, so she decided she might as well stick it out for the final two days.

Odette emptied overflowing ashtrays on the coffee table, sure sign Karen was no longer in California. By the amount of cigarette butts, Pelican State residents had never read the Surgeon-General's warning. Karen caught the maid staring at her and was about to speak but the young girl scurried out of the room, no doubt fearful of being accused of trying to steal the blouse Karen was wearing.

She picked up an outdated *Good Housekeeping* with a blooming Princess Di and her sons on the cover. Monaco and death were years away. She would give Bo fifteen more minutes - then what? The day stretched before her as empty as her life had been before coming to Bayou Vieux.

Suddenly the front door clattered open and Tank rushed in as if chased by a pack of werewolves.

"Miz Benoit, you come quick! Me, I take you to bayou, yes?"

Annoyed, she threw her magazine onto the table. "Did Bo send you to tell me he wasn't coming?"

"No, ma'am, I no talk to Bo Boudreau. Telemaque, he be plenty sick. He not come today. He ask me to get you *quick!*"

"Why does he want me? What's the matter with him?"

"Grandpere, he take real sick last night. Tell grandmere it be gris-gris. He go all frou-frou after supper and when he in bed he dream devil come to he room and pull out all he teeth." Tank's small body shook as he told of his grandfather's illness.

"He probably just ate something that disagreed with him, Tank. I'm sure he'll be fine."

"Why you not listen, ma'am? I tell you grandpere; he dream he teeth be out!"

"So? It was just a dream." Karen half-listened, angry at Bo's failure to show. Probably decided she was too much trouble to waste his time."

"Dat dream mean somebody *die! Soon!* One night old Papile Prideaux dream it and never wake up."

Karen stared at the child, exasperated. "Then how do you know that's what he dreamed?"

"Witch Marie Osey get real mad at Papile one night and fix he with congo snake powder, so he dream he teeth be gone. Next day be dead," the boy finished triumphantly.

Hopeless. But if Telemaque really was sick *somebody* better help. Tank fixed pleading eyes on her.

The day was already wasted.

"Where does he live? Do I need my car?"

Tank beamed. "Yes'um, we take car. Tank's feet, dey be plenty sore from walk over." He held out a grimy, calloused foot. The kid stopped at nothing.

She paused as she passed Lou at the desk, then kept going. Bo hadn't left a message - why should she?

# Chapter Seventeen

Thrilled by the ride, Tank tuned into a rock and roll station, turning the volume louder and louder till Karen finally shouted over the noise, "I can't drive with all that racket, Tank!" and shut off the radio. Pouting, the boy slid down in his seat, giving only vague responses to Karen's exasperated calls for directions. After the fourth dead end, she realized he was only interested in the ride.

"You don't care about your grandfather; you just want to fiddle with the gadgets in this car, Tank!"

"No, ma'am, you gotta make him better," he mumbled, having just discovered the air conditioner. "Brrr, dat be cold, but come summer dat thing be real good, you bet, lady."

"I won't be here this summer."

"Stop!" he yelled suddenly. "You gotta stop here!"

"What do you mean, *here?* There's nothing here."

They had come to the end of a rutted road almost under water from the bayou's overflow. Squawking chickens scuttled past the car, and a boy who looked to be about eight-years-old sprang out from a dense thicket edging the bayou. The boy zigzagged along the water's edge pushing a wheelbarrow containing a fat baby clad in grimy diapers. The makeshift buggy careened dangerously close to the water's edge as the baby bounced madly about.

"Little boy! Stop racing with that baby before you dump him in the water!" Karen shouted, but the laughing child dashed away before the words were out of her mouth.

Tank giggled. "You spook easy, ma'am. Dat be Tyler Moonie's boys. Dey be web-footed, all nine of dem."

"*Nine?*"

"Nine be nothing. Me, I got six bubbas and four soeurs and every one of us still got our teeth. We go dat way." He pointed to a cow path.

Winding through a jumble of dense, wild cane and broad-based Cyprus trees was a narrow passage, scarcely wide enough for a child to pass through. Discarded tires, bottles, old washtubs and several hundred tin cans littered the way.

"I'm not taking this car through that jungle!"

"Den we walk. Please, lady?" Tank yanked Karen's arm. "Telemaque ain't gonna get no better long as we sit here, hein?"

She looked down at her new jeans and thin-strapped sandals which represented countless hours writing sentimental slop, then at the boy so eager to help his grandfather.

"Go on," she sighed, "I'm right behind you."

"Yippee! Telemaque, he be so happy!"

Tank scrambled out of the car and ran through clumps of ten-foot tall cane.

"Slow down! I don't know where I'm going!" Twisting vines and thorny branches whipped Karen's face and shoulders as she tried to follow the racing boy. She rolled up her jeans to avoid the splatter of mud, and was horrified at the sight of her ruined shoes. For a moment Tank's red-striped shirt was visible through the tangled brush, then he shouted something incomprehensible over his shoulder and disappeared again.

"I can't hear you!" Karen yelled. "If you don't slow down I'm going back without you!"

The threat worked. Tank backtracked until she caught up with him.

"What did you say just then? You were running so fast your words came out like a lot of gibberish."

Tank pointed to a sloping stretch of land covered with swamp waters. A log extended three feet from water to shore. As Karen watched, the log shifted and she stared into the beady, black eyes of an alligator five feet from her mud-drenched shoes. She grabbed Tank's shoulder. "How fast can that thing run?"

Tank shook with laughter. "Hee - hee, dat be old Gonfle."

"What kind of name is Gonfle?"

"Means jaws."

Karen stumbled backward, pulling Tank with her.

"Don't you be worry, ma'am. Gonfle, he be too lazy to chase skinny folk like us. He only go after fat dudes."

"Are there any more like him in there?"

"For sure. Can't hunt 'gators no more so we got 'em crawlin' in de out-houses some nights. Dat ain't no pretty sight, ma'am. Just don't go swimmin' in dis part of de Bogolousa.

"What do you mean, the Bogolousa? What happened to Bayou Vieux?"

"We in po' man land now. Bayou Vieux where rich folk live. Round here everybody poor as snakes."

She paused reflectively. "I saw a parade yesterday. Everyone was dressed up like an Indian. Were you in that parade?"

A look of awe lit up his face.

"No, ma'am, dat be Wild Squa-tou-las. You got to be special, you be in dat bunch. Ain't no Caillou ever be a Squa-tou-las."

"Do they live around here?"

"Squa-tou-las be all over."

"The costumes were expensive. You said everyone around here was poor."

"Dey get dem glad-rags with *voodoo*, lady. Voodoo sends 'em bright feather and jewels."

Tank stopped in front of a ram-shackled lean-to supported on stilts, topped by a roof half-thatched with bamboo and broken slats which wouldn't provide much protection in case of heavy rains. Coated in black tarpaper, a strong wind could blow the rickety structure down. He pounded on the door. "Grandmere? It be me, Tank! Me and nice lady. She come see ol' Tel, hokay?"

Following the boy into the small shack, Karen was assaulted by the stench of burning wood and something bubbling in a black cauldron on a pot-bellied stove. The only window in the dark room was covered with newspapers, one sheet of which had flapped loose revealing a jagged hole in the glass pane. The immaculately dressed man she knew from the hotel contrasted drastically with the miserable hovel she stood in.

"Why you be here, Tank boy? You mere know where you be?" A tired-looking black woman came up to them tucking wisps of coarse white hair beneath her scarf. "Lady," she said to Karen, "if you be doctor woman, me and Tel, we do just fine. He be drinking sea gum, grease and swamp lily. That be good for he insides, bien?"

"You keep quiet, Rie!" The old man lying in bed raised himself on one elbow and waved a crooked finger at his wife. "Miz Karen, she ain't no doctor. She be here 'cause I ask she. Go do you business, you hear, old woman?"

The woman drifted back into the shadows, muttering something Karen couldn't understand.

"Come here, please, lady. You come, yes?" Telemaque croaked.

Karen went to Telemaque's bedside, dismayed by the sight of a matted, oil-soaked fur pelt on his chest.

Tank giggled at her reaction. "That be dead mushrat skin, lady," he whispered. "Best thing for as'ma and everything else. Poor ol' Telemaque, he be going fast. Ol' Doc Jake, he charms ain't working too good. You give him jenson weed, Grandmere?"

"Shut up, boy," Telemaque mumbled. "Ain't nothin' gonna work 'gainst gris-gris." A sly look came into his eyes. "Less'n you can get ol' Tel bristle from dat trouble-makin' hog tonight, boy."

Tank jumped back from his grandfather's bedside. "Aw, Tel, you know Tank can't get you no pig hair! Tank try trick like dat, dose guys get more blood from Tank than dey get from dat hog."

Telemaque's head sank back against the pillow. "Dere be no other way, boy." His eyes fluttered shut.

Karen wanted desperately to be out of this smelly hut with its casual talk of blood-letting. She felt sorry for the old man, but had no idea how to help since he was obviously against taking even an aspirin, preferring his wife's garden variety of medication. Still, she could try.

"I have a car; I could get medicine."

Telemaque rolled his eyes. "Dat won't help, Miz Benoit. "You be good lady to come. You listen to Telemaque, den go far away. Dey got voodoo on you!"

"There's no such thing -" she began before Telemaque cut her off.

"You get mal de tete, yes?"

"If you're asking me if I get headaches, yes, of course; everyone does occasionally, nothing serious."

"You find gris-gris," he stated flatly.

"There was a bag of something in front of my door -" She looked to Tank for help but he was rapidly turning the pages of a 1954 Marilyn Monroe calendar and ignored her. Telemaque shook the boy's arm and Marilyn slid to the floor.

"You put gris-gris out for dis lady, boy?"

"Grandpere! Tank no do dat, you know dat." He jerked away from the old man's gnarled hand. "Man, you sure got mean hold for someone just seen *petite blanc chien*!"

Telemaque sank back onto the bed, exhausted from his efforts. For a moment the only sounds in the room were harsh grunts as he struggled for breath. Rie materialized from the shadows carrying a spoonful of something thick and dark.

"*Buvez,*" she muttered, pouring the foul smelling liquid down Telemaque's throat. He spluttered indignantly, but soon the old man's breathing steadied and his eyes lost their dullness.

Amazing plants grew on Rie's windowsill alongside petunias and marigolds. The old lady nodded triumphantly and slunk back into the shadowy recesses of the room.

Telemaque beckoned to Karen. "You watch out for voodoo queen," he whispered. "Dat she-devil, she got helpers all over - dey be out to get you. You best go back where you come from, you hear, Miz Benoit?"

"What do you mean, 'voodoo queen'?"

"Can't tell no secrets or she spook dis poor black man, comprendez-vous? Next temp me de mort for sure! Gris-gris too strong. Mal happen, hein." He slipped into a rapid patois too jumbled for Karen to follow.

"Slow down, Telemaque; I can't understand you."

The old man sighed and closed his eyes.

Tank shifted impatiently "Voodoo powerful strong. Maybe ol' Tel be dead." Suddenly Telemaque bolted upright and pointed a crooked finger at his wife. "Rie, you get doll, *vitement!* You see dis, Miz Benoit, *puis vous croyez.*"

Rie reached under her husband's bed and brought forth a crudely made cloth doll stuck with pins. Strands of blond hair were mixed in with the yellow yarn that passed as hair, and a piece of yellow, poppy-print material was wrapped around the doll's tiny waist. Karen snatched the bizarre object from Rie's hand and ripped the missing piece of her blouse off the doll. "Where did you get this?"

Tank looked like he wanted to cry. "It be me, ma'am. Voodoo doll outside you door. Me, I give it to Telemaque. Somebody out to get you, but dey get ol' Tel first."

"'Cause I try an' help, lady," Telemaque said quietly.

"All the silly charms and potions in the world aren't going to hurt me. Or you, Telemaque! How can you be so reasonable at the hotel, then act like this? You just have a cold," she added scornfully.

Hurt glazed the old man's eyes and he turned to the wall, mumbling vague, unrecognizable phrases.

"I can't hear what you're saying."

"I say you get out, lady! Me, I try help and you laugh. Me be like dis 'cause of you, now you not believe me - so I say *get out!*" He closed his eyes.

His wife shoved Karen toward the door. "You go, lady. You hurt Tel - you not help. He have blood-rush 'cause of you. Allez! Allez!"

"I'm sorry if I hurt your feelings, Telemaque," Karen said quietly, "but if *I* feel sick I go to a doctor and you should too."

"Doc Jake be good doctor," Tank said.

"He's a *witch* doctor!"

Tank shrugged. "He be good Witch Doctor."

"Oh, forget it." She was getting nowhere. "If I can help, let me know." Disgruntled, Karen walked quickly to the door. Rie called after her. "Don't you be calling Doc Jake, ma'am! He put hex on you!"

"Then I'll just have to hex him back, won't I?" Karen yelled over her shoulder as she stepped gingerly down the wooden steps, trying to avoid broken boards. She was pleased to hear Tank clattering after her; perhaps the boy had some sense in him after all.

Once on solid ground she said in a muted voice "You brought me here just to scare me with your voodoo, didn't you, Tank? Where'd you learn all that stuff, anyway? Do they teach voodoo in schools down here?"

"Don't go to school," Tank muttered. "School ain't fun. Stay home, earn money. *Little* kids go to school."

"Where's the one you *should* be going to? Is there a school around here?"

"Down de bayou apiece. We got us waterbus to pick up kids at wharf. We gonna see dem when dey come home, you'll see."

"*We* won't see them. *I'm* going back to the hotel. Sorry I couldn't help, but it appears your grandfather doesn't want my help."

"Maybe you still help, ma'am," Tank said, whistling an off-key tune.

They had come to a clearing where several wooden houses on stilts clung to the levee of Bayou Bogoulousa. Their shapes as identical as California tract homes, each home sported a character of its own. A clothesline draped with hand-made blankets flopped in the breeze at the first house. Muskrat and nutria pelts stacked in a wheelbarrow were in front of the second house, while a scarecrow waved limp arms in the garden of the house next in line. Chubby-cheeked toddlers, chased by exasperated mothers, were everywhere.

Karen turned to Tank. "How do we get back to my car?"

"I show you ma'am, but first-"

"But first nothing! I'm going home!"

"You want to know where Bo be today, right, ma'am?"

Tank ran up the wooden steps of one of the shacks before Karen could stop him. This house had a large water-filled washtub in the front yard. Dark shadows swam beneath the surface with an occasional ugly head emerging from the murky water.

"Miz Boudreau?" Tank hammered on the screen door. "Hey, ma'am, it be Tank."

"Tank - no!" Karen cried. Too late. A handsome, wrinkled woman in her fifties opened the door, sweeping puffs of dust down the stairs with a home-made broom. Her tan was as deep as Bo's.

"Alors, Tank, you think maybe you wake de dead? You think maybe Alex and me be deaf, oui? Come in, 'fore you pound a hole in dat screen."

"Bonjour, Miz Boudreau, me, I got surprise. Come on lady," he hollered down to Karen. "It be okay, dey wanna see you."

"Well, I don't want to see them," Karen hissed back, hoping her voice wouldn't carry into the house.

"Ain't polite to say no to folk what ask you in," the boy retorted. "Come on!" he darted into the house. Karen could have cheerfully rung the little scoundrel's neck, but feeling responsible followed him up the stairs.

From the outside the cottage looked as if a good wind might knock it over, but inside the walls were solid cypress, maybe capable of withstanding hurricanes. The main room was lighter than Telemaque's dark shack because of four good-sized windows. Bright yellow curtains created coziness. A closed door led to the rest of the shotgun house. A black and white television and a CB radio sat side by side on a table, pitting *Gilligan's Island* against Zydeco. Tank plopped down in front of the television, giving new meaning to the term 'zombie'. A spinning wheel stood in a corner of the room; a multi-colored table-cloth, bright pillows and an intricate wall hanging showing men casting nets into water gave evidence of the busy wheel. A handsome handmade rug lay on the floor in front of an orange sofa and two matching chairs. Next to the woven tapestry hung magazine cutouts of the Eiffel Tower, the Arc d'Triumph and the Moulin Rouge. A picture of Jesus Christ was tacked on the wall above the sofa, and lodged between the two orange chairs were burning votive candles and a wooden cross on a prayer-dieu. An eight-foot long, cypress table extended from the tiny kitchen which exuded pungent cooking odors, reminding Karen she'd had neither breakfast nor lunch.

"Sure smell good, Miz Boudreau!" Tank said. "You got you gumbo in dose pots? Jambalaya? Maybe nice shrimp étoufée, hein?"

"You want to give dat broth a stir you find out, boy, but I better find me twenty-four shrimp in dat pot when I be ready to serve, yes?"

The dark-haired woman glanced shyly at Karen but said nothing.

"Sorry to intrude, Mrs. Boudreau. Tank brought me here but we're just leaving."

Mrs. Boudreau beamed a smile displaying a few missing teeth. "You maybe dat lady staying at de hotel?"

Karen nodded, wishing she were there now.

"My son, he be tellin' me 'bout you. You stay for supper, yes? Bo like dat."

"I'm sorry, we can't -" Karen began, but the woman immediately added two plates to the table set for eight, then returned to chopping carrots, turnips, okra and peppers, hurling them into various pots.

"Alex, mon mari, he be glad you eat here, too, lady. He be sleeping now," she said, nodding toward the closed door. "He catch him one fine crop of catfish early morning, den come home and go zzzz. You want catfish for you mere, Tank?'

Tank licked his lips. "I be fou dans le tete if I say no, Miz Boudreau."

"Tien, dey be in yard, mon petit. You grab you one when you go home, yes?"

Karen looked at the ten plastic dishes on the table. "Will your son be eating here tonight, Mrs. Boudreau?" If the woman said yes, Karen would be out of the house in seconds, having no intention of facing Bo after what he had pulled.

"Which one, lady? Me, I got five p'tit boug boug home, not counting Bo who be in and out all de time." Her voice grew confidential. "Bo be birthing Lala now in Vacherie. Dat girl, she never gonna have dat bebe if she don't eat right. Me, I tell her swallow five egg yolks but damn if she don't throw dem right back up."

So *that* explained Bo's absence.

"All dat trouble just to have a bébé. Me," Bo's mother continued proudly giving the room another vigorous sweeping, "dey come out like lapins!"

"Bo's with her now?"

"He go minute he get off work. Alex, he be plenty mad Bo not help him trap muskrat and catch shrimp. Dat boy, he never here. Make Alex damn mad. Say Bo all de time messin' with books."

"Bo's father didn't want him to go to medical school?"

"He want Bo home, make plenty money trapping. But me, I want him be Doc. Doc Boudreau," she grinned. "Ici rien, nobody go to college - you gotta be smart, you do dat. You go sit on porch, lady, I fix good drink, yes?"

Tank held the door open for Karen. "Allez, lady, we go watch for school boat while we wait, yes?"

Doubting her sanity, Karen allowed herself to be led to the porch. As she rocked tentatively at first, she gradually relaxed to the point where she felt lazy and peaceful staring out at the misty bayou in spite of the fact that she had been tricked again. "You knew this, didn't you, Tank? You knew that's why Bo didn't meet me at noon."

"You not like Miz Boudreau? You not like see Bo?"

"I swear you're as slippery as a fish out of water."

"Dat be catfish, ma'am - and me, I never be dat slippery!"

Long after Bo's youngest brothers had tumbled off the school boat and joined Tank and the others playing kick-the-can, Karen sat and watched the setting sun. Candles and lanterns appeared in flickering chorus on the porches of the little village, each soft glow competing with hundreds of fireflies dancing in the lingering dusk. Alex, Bo's father, a tall, wiry man with snapping black eyes and hair the color of steel, joined them on the porch as did several men in the neighborhood, relaxing while their wives cooked supper.

Karen half-dozed, half-listened as the men bragged of the day's catch. Muskrat season was drawing to a close and Alex had taken the day off to trawl for catfish which he traded for a hefty turtle tethered to a stake in the yard. The men chatted and argued good naturedly in a patois too fast to follow. Bo still hadn't arrived and Doucette, his mother, wouldn't let Karen help in the kitchen so she decided to just relax and try to decode the banter going on around her. No one was particularly concerned about Lala's labor difficulties. Everything would be 'hokay' was the general consensus, and talk shifted to more important things like baseball and pirogue racing.

After a time, the children were called to dinner, and several of the brothers drifted off to their own suppers prepared by their wives, any of whom could rival the finest chefs in New Orleans, according to their husbands. Karen and Tank joined the Boudreau family at the long, wooden table heaped high with fried catfish, gumbo, boiled vegetables, garfish balls, a hot sauce which brought tears to Karen's eyes and a magnificent assortment of homemade breads, jellies and pies. No one had turned off the TV and every once in a while a news item would silence the table, but most of the time the room was filled with non-stop, noisy babble.

Karen learned that Bo's five younger brothers helped their father trapping, skinning and oystering. Ulysses, 18, and Henri, 17, worked side by side with their father year round and lived by the Cajun motto: '*laissez bon temps rouler*'. They made enough money from the bayou to take care of card games, horse racing and fais-do-dos - Saturday night dances. Book learning wasn't all that important when a man could fill his belly with beer and good food, his house with bebes and a pretty woman, and pockets with winnings from a bourre game.

Bo had other plans which his brothers joked about with underlying pride. Bo's father was silent when they spoke of his oldest son's accomplishments.

The family ambled back to the porch after supper, and twelve-year-old Charles played the accordion, which earned him pocket money at fais-do-dos and weddings.

"Tee Sharle, he pump dat squeeze-box faster den a water-snake chase a swamp rat, hein? Ain't nobody 'round here make music like dat fils."

"Bo, he be pretty good on he guitar," Ulysses said.

"Bo!" Alex snorted. "Who gonna listen to he play when he be doctor?"

"Hey, Sharle," six-year-old Bos yelled, "play de lady '*Saute Crapaud!*'" Henri laughed. "*Tu petit crevette!* She don't want to hear no song 'bout frog losing he tail. Give her love song - play '*Cajun Waltz*'.

Karen glanced at her watch - seven-thirty. She had hoped to return with Bo, but the night was black and he still wasn't home. Doucette jumped to her feet every time there was a noise outside the house.

Karen rose from the rocking chair which had lulled her into a comfort zone. "I'd love to hear more songs but it's getting late and I have to find my way home. Tank, come be my guide. I'm sure your daughter will be fine, Mrs. Boudreau."

Doucette twisted her apron nervously and murmured, "I hope so. Lala, she built like Naomi. Naomi, she got herself three fat kids. Dey all be big bébé and long time coming, but dat Lala, she never listen. I tell her she gonna have bad time birthing 'cause she asked she five-year-old niece, Ti-ti, to comb she hair for her - she say she belly too fat to reach around. Lady, she be fou in de head! Combing hair 'fore bébé come bad luck! Dat *alway* spell big trouble for birthing. She be lucky dat bébé don't come out with hoofs on he feet!"

How can you argue with stubborn superstition? "I'm sure she'll be all right," Karen repeated. "And her hair will look beautiful. Let's go, Tank."

The boy had been quiet during the evening. "Lady, we talk outside, okay?" Karen nodded, wondering what ordeal she was in for now. She turned to the others. "Goodbye and thank you again. It's been a wonderful day."

"It be dark out," Alex said. "I get you something." He disappeared into the house. A mournful chorus of bullfrogs could be heard from the swamp.

"Hey, Ulysses, *laplie tombe ouaouaron chante*," Henri said

Karen looked to Ulysses for translation.

"Old Cajun saying, 'when rain falls, bullfrogs sing," he responded. "Old Falfi must be kicking de bucket," Tank said. Karen said nothing, remembering Telemaque's prophecy.

Alex came out of the house with a flashlight. "Dis be for you, lady. Bo, he bring it back."

"Good idea. I can certainly use it. Goodbye, and thank you for everything."

The Boudreaus assured Karen she would always be welcome, with or without Bo. She wished today had been *with* Bo.

# Chapter Eighteen

When they reached the bottom of the stairs Karen grabbed Tank's shirt before he could slip away. "Don't you dare leave me again or you're going to be in big trouble! Do you understand?"

"Yes'um, I understand. But I ain't be leaving you, ma'am, I be telling you something." He moved closer and Karen prepared herself for another outrageous statement when young Charles yelled from the porch. "Hey, lady, watch out for *loupgarou!*"

"Let's go, ma'am, *vitement!*" Tank grabbed Karen's arm and tried to pull her toward the open field.

"Hold on, Tank," she said, forcing the boy to stand still. "Charles said loup-garou. I know what that means. Is he really naive enough to think there're werewolves around here?"

"Ain't none here," Tank replied, fidgeting uneasily. "Dey all be down at Bayou Goula where dey hold dem dances."

"What dances?"

"We gotta go, ma'am," he said urgently. "Maybe Sharle, he be right. Maybe some be 'round here." He peered into deep shadows cast by the flashlight, its beam reflecting a heavy mist rising from the bayou. Karen pulled her jacket tighter as she scanned the thick grass for alligators on the prowl. The distant laughter of children playing late night games was comforting as she flashed the light along the ground. Suddenly Tank seized the flashlight and aimed it toward the tops of the trees. Spanish moss hung limp in the still air. The night was oppressive even in the February cool.

"What are you looking for?"

"Like he say, ma'am, loup-garou," Tank said as if speaking to a child.

"There are *no such things*, and if you don't stop talking like that you can walk home! I mean it, Tank, I'll find my own way back to the car."

"Dey bad, ma'am. Dey bite you, you be one, too."

She stared at him speechlessly. "You're driving me batty talking about ghosts and voodoo and werewolves. While you're at it you might look for zombies and mummies and vampires. They're probably hiding here, too."

"Yes, ma'am, I be looking for dem, too," he said solemnly.

"Give me that!" She grabbed the flashlight. "Where's my car? You're going back with me, shouldn't have let you talk me into this in the first place." She seized the boy's hand and walked to where she thought she'd parked the car. "Show me where you live so we can tell your mother where you're going."

"What about Telemaque?"

"What about him?" She slapped a mosquito. The croak of bullfrogs had become louder and the nearby hoot of an owl made them both jump. The boy stared up at Karen tearfully.

"Telemaque need hog bristle. Me, I *have* to get dat thing, ma'am, or my grandpere, he die for sure."

"No hog bristles. He's not going to die."

"He *die*, ma'am!" The little boy began to shiver and cry uncontrollably, his thin arms rattling at his side.

"Stop it! Just stop it right now." Karen wrapped her jacket around Tank, then fished a tissue from her purse. "Blow!"

He blew noisily into the tissue and looked slyly up at her. "You gonna help get dat hog bristle, lady?"

She paused long enough for him to start crying again. "Damn, we'll see," she muttered in frustration.

Tears vanished, he grabbed her hand and dragged her through leg-lashing bushes along a trail too narrow to be called a path.

"For God's sake, Tank, slow down!"

"You want you car, yes?"

"Not if I have to break a leg to get it!" she panted.

He doubled his pace.

Low-lying branches beat at her face and tore her clothes as they crashed through prickly brush and low-hanging vines. If werewolves *were* around they'd probably be scared off by the raucous race through pot-holes and sludge. The flashlight bobbed wildly up and down the marshland, capturing the red-eyed glare of small animals in their path.

Suddenly Tank stopped as if the next step would send him over a cliff, and Karen crashed into him. They had reached the clearing where the car was parked. Sending a quick skyward thank you, she ran to the car and unlocked the door. "Get in, quick! I can't wait to get back to that sorry excuse for a hotel!"

"What 'bout Tel?"

"We can talk about him on the way home."

Tank clung stubbornly to the door, refusing to be coaxed inside.

"Please, Tank, it's late."

"You let my grandpere die."

"He'll be all right, I promise you."

"*No!*"

Karen was desperate, ready to promise anything to get him in the car. She paused, then said brightly. "Would you like to go to California?" Maybe the boy had a short memory.

"Where dat?" he asked suspiciously.

"A lovely place when the sun shines all the time. I live by the beach. If you get in the car you can come visit me."

His grip on the handle relaxed. "When dat be?"

She hesitated. "Whenever your mother says you can." Seeing he was mulling over the offer she rattled on, "Surfing, building sand castles, Disneyland -"

Tank's face lit up. "You mean Disney World? You take me to Disney World?

"It's the other one, Tank. Even better!"

Tank couldn't get in the car fast enough.

Karen drove slowly along the one-lane road, aware of the closeness of the bayou on her right. The thicket became denser between road and bayou until finally they left the swamp land. Tank was quiet as they lurched over the bumpy lane. They came to a fork she didn't remember.

"Which way?"

Tank pointed to the left. "Dat way."

"You're positive?" There were no lights in either direction.

"I be positive."

If the road led nowhere - or to places she'd rather not be - she'd turn back and take the road to the right.

She drove a short distance then caught her breath at the sight of an immense fire several hundred yards away.

"Stop de car, lady," Tank yelled, flipping off the headlights. The car skidded crazily.

"Don't *ever* do that again! I can't see a damn thing." She switched on the head beams. In the distance she could see moving figures silhouetted against the huge fire. Smaller flares bobbed around the bonfire like satellites circling the sun. "Where have you taken me? This isn't the main highway."

"We be at voodoo ceremony."

"Are you serious?"

"You not take Tank to Disney World. Tank be fou in de tete to believe dat!"

Karen sat on her hands to keep from slapping him. "Forget it, I'm not getting out. I'm driving straight back to -" was all she said before the boy yanked open the car door and fled into the night.

"You don't care!" he shouted over his shoulder. "You don't care if Grand-pere die! I get hog bristle so Tel, he don't die!"

Tank zigzagged across the field toward the fire. Gnashing her teeth, Karen tied her scarf over her head, grabbed her purse and flashlight and raced after him.

# Chapter Nineteen

$S$he was at the edge of a wide field. The ground was more solid than the boggy soil by the bayou; hopefully there was no marshland in which to sink ankle-deep. If Tank's siblings were like him she could understand why his parents stayed out of the picture.

She reached the outskirts of the crowd milling about the bonfire and looked for the boy. Exotically dressed men and women wandered about, babbling excitedly. She saw a few white faces among the mostly dark-skinned assembly, all wearing party-like expressions, probably planning to chant a few incantations, then get down to the business of having fun. Telemaque's hog bristles were probably non-existent. Animal sacrifices were a thing of the past, even in rural places like Bayou Bogolousa.

Karen saw Tank darting through the crowd and ran toward him, but her path was blocked by a mammoth woman who refused to budge. It was like scaling the Himalayans to get around her and by the time she reached the other side Tank was gone.

Her chase led her to a courtyard bordered by life size statues missing a few heads, hands and arms, and mounted on six-foot high pedestals: an army of maimed giants. Beyond the courtyard were the ruins of what had been a magnificent plantation, the few remaining columns supporting what was left of a gable roof centered over a huge room, now open to the elements. Much of the marble flooring was intact, the decayed areas given over to hard dirt. Torches lit up the once elegant chamber, casting elongated shadows into invisible corners. Most of the cultists had assembled in this ghostly arena, while others still straggled in.

A low, rhythmic beating of drums came from the center of the room while revelers, mesmerized by the relentless pounding, swayed to the cadence. It would not be impossible to succumb to the spell of the drums in these broken ruins.

Tank scooted in sight again, close enough for Karen to grab his shirt. "Let me go!" he shrieked, struggling to free himself.

"We're going home, Tank!"

"Jeez, lady, you scare me. I thought you be Doc Jake. He don't like kids hanging 'round here. What you be doing here? You wanna speak to a hant?"

"I've been trying to find you. What do you mean, speak to a 'hant'? Are they going to have a séance?"

"Yes'um. Brother Ben Coker - he talk to he daddy every year on St. John's Eve and he daddy been gone twenty year. 'Course he talk to he daddy every day, anyway." He tapped his head. "Brother Coker, he ain't always home up dere."

The courtyard was filling up and Karen and Tank were pushed to the front by hot, sweaty bodies. Karen visualized the ragged clothes of those around her transformed into extravagant finery of the old South. Several men in the crowd carried torches highlighting shiny, exultant faces. All attention focused on an altar where candles, a wooden cross, large jars, loaves of bread and a glass decanter were meticulously placed. Drums hammered from tree trunks accelerated to a feverish pace till only the whites of their eyes showed in the taut faces of the drummers.

"You ain't seen nothing yet, ma'am," Tank whispered. "You just wait till they *really* be going."

"We're not staying that long. We're going *now!*"

She lost her patience and tried to pull Tank away from the crowd but he was inflexible.

"Can't go yet, lady. Look!" He pointed to a metal crate near the altar. The glow of candles and torches illuminated sharp, yellowish tusks that stuck through the bars. The cage was still for a moment, then shook violently as if whatever was held captive had suddenly awakened. A terrifying clamor arose from the box - a cry halfway between a grunt and a bellow.

"See, lady?" Tank yelled excitedly. "Dat be pig Telemaque need to be rid of voodoo spell!"

Karen stared at the gleaming tusks. "That's a *wild boar!* You can't get hair from that thing - unless you want to be gored!"

"Not *hair*, ma'am- *bristle!*

"Whatever, you can't pluck bristles from that snout. Can't you hear him? He's angry and dangerous!"

"Not now, lady. Later. *Den* I steal bristle. Den we go."

"He's not getting any tamer."

Tank drew his finger across his throat and grinned.

"Oh, no, we're not hanging around here till that animal's slaughtered. We're leaving now!" Karen held tight to Tank and tried to push her way through the crowd which had swelled in the last few minutes. Everywhere she turned she was blocked by a mass of undulating flesh.

As noises from the cage increased, so did the drummers' tempo, quickening the fervor of the people. A man broke loose from the mob and started dancing erratically near the altar. Bared to his waist, a tattered pair of grimy white pants belted with a piece of rope covered the dancer's skinny hips and legs. His emaciated chest was draped with chains and knotted ropes from which hung bones, dice, animal paws, tiny skulls, and dried frogs. His hair, looped and twisted into foot long tendrils, hid amulets and herbs. Tiny bird's nests, dangling from his hair, cascaded down his back, and as he jumped about a steady rain of curios and coins rattled to the floor, scooped up by excited spectators.

"Dat be Doc Jake!" Tank hissed in Karen's ear.

"The so-called *doctor* you wanted for Telemaque?"

"Doc Jake, he cure everything! Bubba Reggis, he step on nail and he foot swell up like football. Doc Jake, he make he drink tea from mashed cock-a-roaches, den Reggie get well. Ol' Doc Jake, he be one fine man, you bet!"

"Sounds more like a death squad."

More worshippers joined the witch doctor on the dance floor, their fierce gyrations affecting those around them. Young girls' and old women's skirts twirled high above glistening limbs. Karen recognized the hotel maid, Dette. She must have sewn Telemaque's voodoo doll, but why? Karen had seen a few ridiculous horror movies in which ill-fated victims writhed in agony after their look-a-like rag dolls were stuck with pins. What had she done to make the maid so angry?

Just as the arena was primed for explosion, the revelers began to chant: "Kulev, Kulev - o, m'ape rele Kulev o -" and the wild tattoo of the drums slowed to a steady, ominous beat. The dancers became sleepwalkers, occasionally animated by violent jerks. Chants grew louder as the crowd shuffled feet in time to the drums. "Kulev, Kulev - o, m'ape rele Kulev - o."

"Dey be bringing back the dead now, ma'am," Tank said in hushed tones. "Dey be saying, 'Serpent, serpent, we call de serpent.' Dere be Mambo," he hissed as a large, black woman solemnly approached the altar. "She be powerful Voodoo queen. Know everything! She be one who put curse on poor Tel."

Dressed in a white flowing robe, the woman strode majestically through the smoke-hazed room toward the altar, her head bound in a foot-high white turban while live snakes writhed around each of her muscular arms. The snakes' eyes glittered and their tongues darted in and out of fanged mouths as the dancers continued to chant "Kulev, Kulev, m'ape rele Kulev - o." The mambo thrust out her arms in crucifix form and the chanting stopped. Then, as she threw back her head and commanded in low, ringing tones, "Kulavo, Kulevo, Dabala-wedo, papa", the possessed dancers made hissing noises and dropped to the ground where they slithered around in the sensuous motion of snakes.

Karen drew Tank closer. Was this the making of some freaky horror movie? She now knew why the woman in white seemed so familiar: she was Odelia, her aunt's housekeeper. As she tried to make sense out of what she was seeing, another woman dressed in white drifted in a somnambulist's trance up to the altar - only this woman wore no turban and her thick, black hair tumbled wildly down her back, her skin so pale as to fade into what was left of a torn and grubby wedding gown. Her open eyes saw nothing; her mouth was slack uttering meaningless grunts.

Astonished, Karen's mouth went dry, for the woman swaying before the altar in a zombie-like trance was her aunt, Zelena D'Aquin.

"Let go, lady, you be hurting me!" Tank yelled, trying to squirm away from Karen's rigid grasp. She realized she was fiercely gripping his shoulder for support and relaxed her hold.

"What are they going to do next?"

"They be call de dead," he whispered fearfully, unable to avert his eyes from the frightful sight. He grabbed Karen's hand. "Dis be scary part."

A silence fell as the mambo unwound the snake from her left arm and dropped it into one of the jars on the altar, repeating the action with the other serpent. "Kulevo, Kulevo, Dabala-wedo, papa," Odelia mumbled in low, guttural tones echoed by the crowd as she fell into a trance.

All was quiet save for the hiss of captive snakes and grunts from the boar. Seconds became minutes until finally a tiny, melodic voice came from the mouth of the voodoo queen, reminding Karen of someone she knew yet couldn't give face to. The child that spoke out from the huge woman was lost and crying, "Help me, Mama. Please help me get out, Mama!" Karen's flesh crawled as she heard childish pleas coming from the old woman. The voice was not the voice of an adult imitating a little girl; it was real and heart-breaking. "Will you help me, Mama?" the tiny voice cried again. Someone screamed, others shouted "Amen!" as Zelena D'Aquin sank to her knees.

At that moment a sharp elbow dug into Karen's back, throwing her off balance. She looked back and saw a tall figure pushing his way to the front of the crowd. "Hey, man, quit you shoving!" a huge black man growled, almost knocking Karen and Tank to the ground. Stripped to his waist, bulging muscles glistening from the heat of pressing bodies, the angry man looked as if he could crush with one blow the slender, older man forcing his way to the altar.

Karen ducked to avoid the sweeping glance of Richard D'Aquin, but all his attention was focused on Zelena, still on her knees and swaying in an hypnotic trance. Her uncle swept up his wife in his arms, showing surprising strength for one so fragile looking.

The mambo stepped forward, her eyes filled with rage. "White man fool to tempt powers of Kulev!"

"I'll have you run out of town if you try this again, Odelia! I've told you before to stop interfering with my wife and her problems. Now get the hell out of my way and get rid of that obscene altar before I burn it to the ground!"

D'Aquin started back through the crowd carrying his comatose wife. Frustrated by the loss of their chosen disciple, the agitated mob wouldn't let him through at first, but the look on his face persuaded even the angriest protestor to allow passage. Karen turned away as her uncle stormed past, grateful for the scarf that concealed her blond hair.

Odelia's face was blank, but her eyes burned with the ferocity of a mother tiger as she watched her enemy melt into the shuffling throng.

# Chapter Twenty

The drums began again, softly at first, gradually increasing in tempo until the worshipers began to sway once more, anxious to resume their ritualistic fervor.

Karen tugged at her small charge's hand. "Move, Tank! We're getting out of here!"

"Can't go," he said stubbornly.

"I'm going to pass out if I don't get air!" She dragged the boy through the shuffling mob which was so intent on their rapturous contortions that the couple was able to push through untouched. When Karen finally broke through to the perimeter of the gathering she leaned against a giant statue, not daring to release her grip on Tank, although the boy was twisting and fidgeting as if he'd stepped on a nest of red ants. As she struggled to regain her breath, Karen saw the circle of gyrating bodies part as a stooped, elderly woman limped up to the altar. This time Odelia assumed the voice of a querulous old man. The Voodoo Queen was at it again with her uncanny impersonations.

Karen pressed her cheek against the column, grateful for the feel of the cold marble against her flushed skin. Then she screamed as a hand gripped her shoulder.

"It's okay, Karen, it's me!"

The minute she heard Bo's voice, Karen threw her arms around the man she had become so dependent upon in the last few days, kissing him with such gusto that he lost his balance and fell to the ground, Karen on top.

"Tien, Cherie," he wheezed, "If this is what voodoo does to you we gotta come here more often!"

She burst out laughing, but his second kiss silenced her laughter with a hunger that intensified the longer they kissed. Surrounded by the throbbing drums, their passion seemed a part of the tumultuous night.

At last Karen broke away and rolled to one side. "My God," she gasped, "I guess I *have* been hexed." Contented, feeling their first wild stirrings of love, they lay side by side, hands clasped, gazing up at the dazzling stars blanketing the black velvet sky, impervious to the pulsating babble around them

Finally, Bo leaned over and kissed Karen gently on her forehead. "You know, Cherie," he murmured, "this is what I've been waiting for ever since I squeezed your pale little hand on the airplane, but I think we better find that little scamp before he turns us all into zombies."

She scrambled to her feet. "Oh my God, I forgot about Tank! He got away again." She started running back through the crowds till Bo caught up with her.

"Slow down, Karen, he's not going anywhere, and you might cause a bigger riot if your start shoving your way around. We'll find him, just take it easy."

She eased her pace and let him take her hand. "How'd you find me, anyway?" she asked in an effort to be calm, although she was sure everyone around them could hear the pounding of her heart above the drums.

"I just spent the last two hours looking for you. Rie told me what Tel wanted, and knowing Tank I thought you'd end up at the ceremony. Shouldn't be here, Cherie, these crowds can get rowdy."

"Tell me about it! They must all be high on drugs."

"Some of them are, only not the trendy, California kind. These drugs would send the average celeb screaming to AA. Let's find the kid then I'll take you both home."

"My car's here, I can't ride back with you."

"Get it tomorrow. I'll drive you back in the morning."

Karen stood still, oblivious to the wild excitement around her. They were both shouting to be heard. "No. I'm meeting my aunt tomorrow at ten."

"You still want to meet her after what just happened? That woman at the altar *was* your aunt, wasn't she?"

"I guess she never got over her daughter's death."

"Don't get mixed up in this, Karen, you don't know what these people are capable of. Your aunt isn't mentally stable. She can't be to fall for that hoodoo stuff."

She glared at Bo, her guard up again in spite of the fervor they just shared. "I don't need you to tell me what to do, and I'd appreciate it if you had respect for my family. I just spent the day with yours and they weren't exactly normal!"

"At least we agree on that. Sorry we missed the picnic."

"Your sister! Is she all right? Did she have the baby?"

"Nine pounds, three ounces. Typical Boudreau bébé. She's fine. The whole *abnormal* family is over there now."

Karen paused, ashamed of her outburst. "I'm sorry, Bo, I shouldn't have said that. Your family is one of the nicest bunch of people I've ever met. I envy you."

Suddenly Tank sprinted past, his face flushed with excitement. Bo darted after him and grabbed the hysterical boy before he got lost in the teeming crowd.

Tank squirmed and tried to escape Bo's firm grip. "Lady! The hog bristles! You promised!"

"I did *not* promise, Tank. We're going home!"

"*No!!!*" he screamed. "I be staying! Gotta help Tel!"

Looking into the boy's fear-filled eyes, Karen realized what it had cost him to come to this place. His life revolved around frightening spells, superstitions and the bogeymen that threatened disaster twenty-four hours a day - all of which were as real to him as the mindless verses she penned at home. Yet he had braved zombies, loup-garous and very tangible alligators to help his grandfather.

"Bo, you saw Telemaque. He's convinced someone's hexing him, and a boar's bristle is the only thing that will make him well again."

"You gonna get it for me, Bo?" Tank implored. "You be getting that hog bristle for ol' Tel so he be well again?"

Bo looked back at the restless crowd. The ominous chanting sounded like the beating of a heart. He squatted beside Tank. "You trust me, don't you, Tank?" The boy stared at the ground. "Do you?"

"I guess," he finally mumbled.

"Do you trust me to make Tel well?"

"You can't."

"Remember when I got the nail out of your brother's foot and he could walk again?"

"Tank!" Karen spluttered. "You said the witchdoctor saved your brother's foot!"

"Doc Jake *coulda* helped Reggie - he do plenty other good stuff!" the boy protested.

Bo laughed and ruffled the boy's hair. "That's okay, Tank, but now you owe *me* one. How about I take you and Karen home? I promise I'll go straight back to Telemaque and make him well - just like I made Reggie well. Deal?"

"Well - okay," the little boy said slowly, "but if Tel stay sick you gotta come back and get dat hog bristle!"

Bo raised his right hand. "Scout's honor."

Karen looked at her watch. Nine-thirty. "Bo, your job! You'll be late."

"I talked Lou into working overtime. I might have to sit for Telemaque tomorrow; doesn't sound like he'll be going in just yet." He put his arm around Tank. "What do you say, kid? Had enough voodoo for one night?"

"I guess," Tank mumbled.

"Then let's find Karen's car."

Tank was asleep when they deposited him with his not-too-concerned parents, then Karen followed Bo's rusty pickup back to the hotel. They said goodbye at her door, and she braced herself for a cousinly kiss. Away from the intoxicating mood of the night, she was sure they'd return to the polite rapport she considered necessary for her remaining stay in Bayou Vieux.

"I'm sorry we never had our picnic, Karen. I wanted to show you the beautiful side of Louisiana. Sure you won't change your mind and stay longer?"

"You know I have to go back on Wednesday."

"If you can't, you can't." He pulled her to him and his kiss was anything but cousinly. More than anything at that moment. Karen wanted to free him from the rough cotton of his shirt and let her hands explore the muscular body beneath. When they finally broke apart they were both breathless. Bo shook his head. "Oh, Cherie, where have you been all my life?"

"Waiting," she said softly and meant it.

"Guess I better see if I can get Telemaque back on his feet," Bo said reluctantly. He took pencil and paper from his breast pocket and scribbled numbers. "That's my cell phone. Call me tomorrow. If I don't answer, leave a message. Promise me?"

She hesitated. "I'll call after I've seen my aunt. I'm not sure what condition she'll be in."

"Don't worry, Cherie, your aunt's not the first person who tried to hook up with a dead person around here. The woods are full of them."

"If you ask me this whole damn state's bonkers," she laughed.

"Now you're the jolie femme I want to spend my life with. Can I talk you into taking a late supper tomorrow night? I'll bring some of Mama's King

Cake. Maybe you'll find the plastic baby doll, then you *won't* be able to leave on Wednesday. It's tradition for the finder to give the next Mardi Gras party."

"I don't know what my aunt's planned for tomorrow night - or even if she'll be all right after tonight." She paused. "Maybe the evening won't run too late."

"I'll keep my fingers crossed."

They kissed again, then Karen stepped quickly into her room before she did something she might regret.

# Chapter Twenty-One

Zeus howled from somewhere within Vencus as Karen tentatively rapped on the front door at ten o'clock on Tuesday morning. She pounded the brass eagle several times, stirring nothing but an irate dog. Was this the final brush-off before her return to California? She pushed damp hair back from her forehead. The light mist became heavier the longer she waited. Swift moving, black clouds replaced the leisurely white ones which promised a fair day. Old Falfi must be dead if there was any truth to Tank's prophecy.

Lightening whitewashed the sky, followed by a blast of thunder heralding a downpour. A skittish breeze blew the rain toward Karen, drenching her in spite of the overhead portico. She pulled her jacket tighter, hammered on the door, and was finally rewarded by the sound of approaching footsteps. Minus snakes, but scowling as usual, Odelia opened the door, Karen pushed her way inside the dry hallway.

"Good morning, Odelia, I was about to start looking for a life raft. My aunt is expecting me at ten-thirty."

Karen gave no indication that she was aware of the housekeeper's bizarre, duel life style, and Odelia was her normal surly self as she led Karen into the library.

No friendly fire to greet her, and Karen said nothing - let Odelia make the first move.

The standoff lasted sixty seconds. "Tell my aunt and uncle I'm here, will you?" Karen asked, furious that she had caved. "They must not have heard me knock."

"Mr. D'Aquin not here. He be showing guests around town".

"But I thought -"

"You thought what?" Odelia cut in sharply, daring Karen to oppose her obvious lie.

"Nothing," Karen muttered, wisely avoiding further confrontation.

"I fix lunch," Odelia intoned triumphantly and left Karen to her churning thoughts.

The room was musty. A chilling humidity induced by years of heavy rains and endless mists pervaded the very books the walls were built to protect. She stooped to study a section of worn volumes near the floor: children's books. She withdrew '*Peter Rabbit*' and opened it to a dog-eared page. A rank, moldy odor clung to pages long ignored, and a wreath of dried flowers fell to the floor. A forgotten memory slipped into place: Easter, a gift on a sunny morning. Returning Peter to his shelf she withdrew another children's book and found a dried spray of holly. Christmas. Her eyes filled with tears.

"Dat be one of Miz. D'Aquin's special books."

Karen dropped the book. "I didn't hear you come in." She picked up the book and brushed off its cover, stirring up years of dust and cobwebs. "It's not a first edition if that's what you mean."

"All Miz D'Aquin's things be special," Odelia snatched the book from Karen and placed it firmly back on the shelf.

Determined to be pleasant - she was obviously dealing with a disturbed person - Karen said nonchalantly, "Did you want something, Odelia?"

"Miz D'Aquin be sleeping. She see you when she wake up."

"We had a ten-thirty appointment. It's almost eleven."

"Miz D'Aquin, alway sleep late after she be out night before." Odelia stated with such animosity that Karen knew she had been seen the previous night. "She be seeing you when she wake up." The housekeeper started to leave, then turned back and laughed unpleasantly. "You friend, he got powerful magic to make ol' Tel better so quick. Don't need no charms like Doc Jake. Wonder how good he magic be next time."

"How did you know about Telemaque's illness? I didn't even know you knew him."

"There be no secrets in Bayou Vieux. Everybody know everybody here."

"Then you should know that Bo is a doctor, not a magician. He doesn't believe in superstitious cures - or curses."

"Voodoo strong. If Telemaque be better, it be magic."

Unwilling to further antagonize the woman, Karen changed the subject. "If it's not raining I'm going to take a walk while I'm waiting for my aunt. Please show me to the back yard."

Frowning, Odelia led Karen past the kitchen to a glassed-in porch crowded with begonias and ferns.

She had been in this room before, she knew it. A white, rattan lawn swing with dark blue cushions once faced the lawn where a small child could sit for hours and watch the rain beat down the leaves of the rhododendron bushes. The swing was dark green now, and the cushions pink and green like a tropical garden. She sat in the swing, reliving the gentle back and forth motion, and told herself she was wishing for the moon. She had never been here before, every conservatory has a garden swing. A coincidence, that's all.

She opened the porch door to a back yard blazing with roses, hydrangeas, azaleas and magnolia trees. A rhododendron bush pushed against the porch window just as her muddled mind had recorded it. Carpet-like grass sparkled from the recent rain. The glistening fairyland was threatened by shadowy puffs marching across the sun, promising future showers.

Feeling as if she were being watched, Karen glanced at a window on the second floor but saw only closed drapes. She hesitated, unable to shake off the sensation of eyes following her, then finally decided to walk down a stone path leading through a bower of dense trees. Pushing aside low-hanging vines and tangled brush, she poked her way to the bank of a bayou.

The water lay still and foreboding, an occasional frog's croak or loon's cry the only sounds breaking the spell of a timeless world. A snow-white heron rose from the moss-draped cypresses and dove toward her. Startled, Karen stepped back to avoid being gored by its sharp beak, but the bird swerved at the last minute, hovered briefly in space, then gently descended to a landing site on a mass of lily pads. A painting by Monet - and a scene from her dreams.

Suddenly she heard someone gasping for air, struggling to breath, directly behind her and whirled about but no one was there. Images raced through her head - someone slipping and sliding along the muddy banks of the bayou guided by a full moon. She heard crying. A child? Lights bobbed through the thicket surrounding the bayou and the area was flooded with lights and jumbled voices. And then the visions were gone, as quickly as they had come. The heron took flight and Karen was alone, remembering another time, the terror, the dread of the unknown.

The child's cry echoed in her mind as she hurried up the path to where Odelia watched her on the sloping lawn of Vencus.

"Something be wrong?" Odelia asked with a peculiar smile on her face.

Karen steadied her breathing. "Not really, I'm not used to bayous."

"Swamp full of things you see nowhere else."

"Actually it was quite calm down there," Karen lied. "Probably a nice day for a boat ride."

"Tainted Kietre sometime be dere. Miz D'Aquin, she never let Zeus or Odin go down dere."

"Is Odin another dog?" The housekeeper gave a slight nod. "And what is Tainted Kietre?"

"He be part man - part alligator. Eats live things."

'Squirrels and birds?"

"People."

Karen raised an eyebrow. "Another Big-Foot?"

"Tainted Kietre live in swamp before you be born. Tainted Kietre be dere forever."

The housekeeper returned unhurriedly to the house. Subdued, Karen followed her, wondering what she had actually seen in the bayou.

Once again, she was left alone in the library.

With the need to vent her frustration, Karen dialed Bo on her cell phone but got his recorded message: "I'm not able to come to the phone right now but please leave your number and a message."

"Hi Bo, this is Karen. I still haven't seen my aunt and I've been here an hour. Don't know about tonight but I'll talk to you later." She laid her phone on the table next to her in case he called back right away.

The rain had begun again, darkening the library room so Karen switched on a lamp and selected *The Hound Of Baskerville* from D'Aquin's huge collection. Delighting in the irony of her choice, she was prepared to wait all night. Whatever heat warmed the house failed to reach the library, so she concentrated on the story to keep warm.

She had reached Doyle's delicious description of the Yorkshire moors when a snuffling by her side startled her and she turned to stare into the vacant, rheumy eyes of Zeus, the Great Dane, his muzzle inches from her face. She remained motionless as a deep rumble sprang from the beast's throat. Threads of drool dripped from his mouth as he strained against her shoulder. Remembering her aunt's description of the gentle creature, she massaged his shoulders, murmuring, "Nice boy, nice Zeus, next time don't charge while I'm reading about maniacal dogs." Her calm voice worked well - he submitted to her caress.

A thin cry came from upstairs followed by a crash of thunder and lightning. Zeus whimpered, tail tucked between his legs, and lumbered out of the room. The cry came again, more of a moan this time, impossible to ignore. Karen put down her book and followed Zeus to stairs leading to the second floor.

A door was ajar near the second floor landing. "Is everything all right?" Karen called from the hall. The crying stopped. "Aunt Zelena, is that you?" A clap of thunder was the only reply. Zeus staggered out to greet her, his odd, loping gait no longer a threat. She patted his broad shoulders, grateful for the slobbering kisses.

"You may come in," a voice called.

Karen paused, uncertain of what might be waiting for her.

"Come, come, my dear, I know you're there. I won't bite."

She hesitated, then entered a room lit only by candles stationed on either side of a canopied bed. A waxen face stared up at her, animated by darting eyes. This was the same woman Karen had met at the cemetery, yet vastly different from the haunted creature at the voodoo ceremony, pleading for a sign from her dead child.

"Give me your hand, Karen."

Zelena sounded sane enough. Karen extended her hand, Zeus shuffling restlessly by her side.

"I see you've made friends with my poor darling. I told you the other night he wouldn't hurt you. Please excuse my lazy behavior, I had a rather late night."

"I know," Karen said, adding quickly, "Odelia told me."

"And did she tell you where I was?"

"Some kind of a ceremony."

Zelena's eyes stopped wavering and focused on Karen. "It's called a voodoo ritual. I've had headaches and insomnia for years, so I thought I'd try a few native remedies. Since Odelia is highly regarded in that field I decided to see if her ways worked better than medical science."

"And did they?" Karen asked, remembering her uncle's mad dash through the crowds, carrying Zelena's limp body.

"I slept like a baby afterwards."

"I heard someone crying. Are you all right?"

"I'm fine now that you're here. I was reliving sad memories - part of Odelia's therapy.' She struggled to a sitting position. "Will you hand me my robe, please? It's on the chaise lounge. I don't think I'll bother dressing for lunch, Richard won't be here and you don't mind us girls being sloppy, do you?"

"Of course not, it's better to be comfortable."

Karen crossed the room to pick up a champagne-colored peignoir draped across a settee and was shocked to see another dog, smaller than Zeus but with a great deal more wilder look, rise from behind the furniture. He blocked her way with a menacing growl.

"Well, go on," Zelena insisted. "Hand me my gown."

"Your dog won't let me." The beast advanced toward Karen, snarling as if to attack.

"Nonsense! Show him the whip," her aunt commanded, indicating a riding crop slung across the foot of her bed.

The dog came closer, ears laid back, teeth bared, deep growls erupting from its taut throat. Zeus, provoked by the other dog, staggered to his feet and lurched toward Karen from the other direction. She was trapped between two drooling, agitated monsters.

"Shut up, Odin!" Zelena said sharply. "Zeus! Lie down! For goodness sakes, Karen, show them the whip before you're ripped to pieces!"

"I'd rather not. Can't you control them?"

"Of course, I can. I always do." Zelena struggled out of bed, picked up the riding crop and cracked it over Odin's head. Instantly he ran from the room, followed more slowly by Zeus. She returned the crop to the foot of the bed. "You've got to be firm or they're unruly."

"He looks ferocious."

"Mastiffs can be tamed if you show them who's boss. Odin was abused as a pup. Sometimes he gets out of hand, but he's a good watchdog - once he know who's in command. I hope you're hungry, I always have a colossal appetite after a migraine."

"I'm not making it worse for you, am I?"

"My dear, when you know me better you'll realize I have good days as well as bad. With you here it promises to be a wonderful day. If you'll grant me a few minutes to tend to this shriveled old face I'll join you in the dining room for Odelia's yummy cooking." She wrinkled her nose in pleasure. "I believe we're honored with hush puppies today." A concoction of cooking odors drifted up from the first floor. Zelena slipped thin feet into fluffy mules. "Do you know why Southerners call their heavenly biscuits 'hushpuppies'?"

"No idea."

"The scrumptious things were created before the Civil War. Plantation owners entertained with fish fries. As cooks fried fish in big vats of oil, every hound in the village came begging. One day a cook, anxious to quiet a hungry mutt, scooped out some of the leftover batter from the fish which had plumped up to a golden brown and tossed it to the dog yelling "hush, puppy!" The fried batter created such a stir among the canine population that the cook decided to try one himself, loved it and hush-puppies were born."

"Such a simple explanation," Karen said, wondering how she could have found this pleasant woman to be so formidable.

"As are so many explanations. Let's go downstairs. We'll have lunch, then that talk. I feel in excellent spirits today."

# Chapter Twenty-Two

Odelia's cooking lived up to its reputation, and if the service wasn't as cheerful as it could have been - well, obviously Voodoo queens weren't exactly standup comediennes. After Karen finished off a second glass of wine, she decided the housekeeper was almost appealing, nothing like the fearsome sorceress of the previous night.

The elegant table setting had seduced her into a sense of serenity. Glistening silver on creamy linens surrounded a cut-glass bowl of pink and red sweet-peas and carnations; slender, pink candles in silver holders created a Valentine setting. They lingered over sherry while Odelia cleared the table.

"What a delicious lunch," Karen said sincerely. "What was in the soup?"

"Squirrel. Richard is expert with rifles."

Karen almost choked, seeing briefly the playful creatures she fed on her balcony at home. "I shouldn't have asked."

"And I should have said chicken. What would you like to talk about, Karen? You wrote that you remembered nothing of your early years."

"Let's start with the Children's Home. Why was I there? Was there a fire?"

"I see you've already discovered a few things which makes my task easier."

"Can you tell me why I was at the orphanage?"

"Oh, dear, I wish your uncle were here, Karen. He's much better at this than I."

"Odelia said he's showing your guests around town."

"Forgive us, dear, but that was a small fib. We have no guests. You must have thought it strange, us getting in touch after all these years."

"I want to know the truth about my background."

"Richard isn't here because he can't bear to be around when we discuss your mother. He's very fond of you, but a coward when it comes to the truth. He'll be back for the party tonight - and there *will* be other guests, I can assure you."

"You sound so ominous about my mother."

"If you'd had a normal, parent-child relationship I wouldn't be telling you this at the age of - how old are you, Karen? I've lost track."

"Twenty-one."

"Of course, how could I have forgotten? The age my daughter would have been had she lived. Your mother and I gave birth the same year." She paused. "Elena, was my fraternal twin. Your grandmother thought it precious to give twin sisters sound-alike names. For years we had to wear the same clothes. Elena was gorgeous. Not being identical twins, I can say that in all modesty, but Elena *knew* she was beautiful and played her beauty to the fullest. She was quite vain. This may be painful for you. The truth often is."

"Go on."

"She used to primp for hours in front of the mirror. We were Cajun, dirt-poor, muskrat-trapping, shrimp-baiting Cajuns and your mother hated poverty."

Karen's mind floated to Bo's shack by the bayou. Strange, she and he were of the same background.

Zelena continued, "We had a happy family life - in spite of Elena's frustrations - until our parents died, mother from bearing too many Benoit brats, father from a trapping accident. Elena and I moved to New Orleans for better jobs. We were silly young things, particularly Elena. She discovered boys at a young age and realized she could advance quickly by using sex as a carrot on a stick - sometimes withheld, more often bestowed - and the money she earned with her nightly adventures paid for the silks and satins she felt she deserved."

Karen's legs were like sponges; she couldn't have stood if she tried.

"Are you saying my mother was a prostitute?"

"Would you rather I stopped?"

"Go on. I asked you to tell me."

"With Navy bases so close, New Orleans crawled with sailors out for a good time and your mother saw that they got it. She ate steak while the rest of us had hamburger. And she climbed the ranks while eating that steak. A pity, for she could have met a nice sailor boy and married him - they were there for the taking. But her sights were higher. A certain captain was her goal, married, but that didn't stop your mother. He settled her in a small apartment on Bourbon Street. Their clandestine relationship continued until she got greedy and tried to force the issue by getting pregnant." Zelena took Karen's hand. "The resultant child was you."

Years of building barriers against the outside world had strengthened Karen, so her voice was steady when she asked, "Is there a way I can trace him?"

"Perhaps through DNA, but I can't think why you would want to."

Karen said nothing, fighting to keep back tears as Zelena continued. "My sister's friend took you to an orphanage, claiming to be me. After I married Richard, her friend got in touch with me and told me about you. By then they had released you to foster homes. For years I tried to locate you but always got the runaround. Fortunately, you kept the same name my sister gave you so I finally found you on the internet." She smiled sadly. "Now you have the whole story. I'm sorry it couldn't have been more pleasant."

Karen sat still for a long time, not trusting herself to speak. Finally, she said, "Thank you for telling me. It couldn't have been easy for you."

"You had to know, my dear." Her smile faded as she looked down at their clasped hands. "Where did you get that bracelet?"

Karen twisted the small gold chain. "I almost forgot, a little girl in town asked me to wear it while I'm here. I must return it before I go."

"What little girl?"

"Her mother runs a bed-and-breakfast in town. I was thinking of staying there but changed my mind."

Zelena smiled again. "It's a pretty thing. You must return it by all means."

"I intend to." She stood. "What time shall I be here tonight?"

"Six-thirty. Richard's taking us into New Orleans for a special dinner where he plans to make an announcement which should please you."

Karen forced a smile. Nothing mattered now. "Don't bother to get up, I'll let myself out."

"Before you go, Karen -" Zelena fumbled with the catch on a small pillbox by her plate and took out two pills. "I want you to take one of these now and another in a few hours. It will relax you and I think you need a bit of calming. Just a mild sedative my doctor gives me when he thinks I'm too stressed out. Once in a while it actually works."

"I better not take it now; I have to drive home."

"You won't get a reaction for at least an hour and by that time you'll be home. This has been a dreadful disclosure for you which is why I tried to put it off for so long. Tonight Richard and I will have news of a brighter sort, but I want him with me for that part." She offered Karen the pills again. "Take them and rest up for the evening."

To please her aunt, Karen took a pill, then decided she had to know all the answers. "Aunt Zelena, there was a fire at the St. Francis where I'm staying - about fifteen years ago. What can you tell me about it?"

Zelena frowned. "Why do you want to know?"

"I'm trying to find out why my memory was blocked all these years. The fire might have had something to do with it."

"It was a traumatic time for all of us. Please go now; I'm not feeling well."

"I understand and I'm sorry if I've upset you. I'll see you tonight," Karen said softly and left the room.

# Chapter Twenty-Three

The center of Bayou Vieux was less than a mile from the St. Francis, plenty of time to clear her head before the evening - and perhaps get answers her aunt was reluctant to give.

Karen was almost glad to see the librarian bent over another tome, bringing a sense of normalcy to her chaotic thoughts. She spoke softly to the elderly woman, not wishing to startle her. The library was empty except for two small girls at a nearby table.

"Do you remember me, Mrs. Hester? You said I could look at a few old newspapers in the stacks."

Annoyed at the disturbance, the librarian looked up from her book "You may go in, young lady, we close at four o'clock."

"Thank you, I won't be long."

She walked through the archway into a small, dark, windowless room and groped along the wall until she found a light switch. An overhead bulb cast a muted light on a room filled floor to ceiling with oversized, leather-bound books. Wall-to-wall shelves and free standing stacks overflowed with three-foot long books neatly chronicled according to years.

She pulled down a weighty volume and saw it was a collection of newspapers from May - August, 1965. She returned the book and scanned other volumes, searching for the '80's or '90's. She stopped at Jan - April, 1992, the year of her birth. Her birth certificate listed New Orleans, Louisiana as her birth place, that much she knew. April 22nd through to the 30th announced the arrivals of babies born in and around New Orleans, but no Karen Benoit. She decided to go further back to the late '80's to see if she could find any information about the D'Aquins or even a dirt poor Cajun family named Benoit.

For an hour she flipped through pages describing cotillions, Krewes, scandals and weddings. From time to time she was rewarded with items about balls or parties at Vencus presided over by Mr. and Mrs. D'Aquin - possibly her uncle's parents - and then she hit pay dirt.

The paper was dated June 19, 1989. Spread across three columns on page one of the New Orleans Times-Picayune society section, was a picture of a story-book bride married to Richard Rene D'Aquin - but the bride's name was Elena, not Zelena. A typo? She glanced at the date again: June 19, 1989. This was February. Why would anyone celebrate a wedding anniversary four months early? She read the article carefully. The wedding, a social highlight, took place at Vencus which had been transformed into a 'winter wonderland with white damasked tables dotted amongst carpets of white carnations, while thousands of tiny white lights twinkled through oaks, myrtles and blooming magnolias, and strolling violinists entertained the aristocrats of Louisiana society.' The enthusiastic reporter went on to state that 'The Honorable Louis D'Aquin, a fifth generation D'Aquin, judge of Louisiana's Supreme Court, and wife Felicia honored their only child Richard and his beautiful bride with a never-to-be-forgotten celebration.'

But who was the bride? Her aunt Zelena, or the amazing thought that perhaps her mother was the Elena Benoit as the paper suggested? If so, and the idea seemed as bizarre as the whole town of Bayou Vieux, if there was no typo and the name was correct, why had she been lied to - or the truth omitted - all these years?

She took a deep breath. Did that mean that Richard D'Aquin was actually her father? Was that what this was all about? The big secret they were finally going to divulge? She read through the rest of the papers as far as August 31, 1989, hoping for further revelations of the D'Aquin family, but apart from a brief mention of the newlyweds' honeymoon trip to Acapulco, that was it. There was no mention of any other Benoits at the wedding, and no repeat mention of the bride's name.

She glanced at her watch, surprised to see it was almost four. She switched off the light and hurried back to the main hall and Mrs. Hester's scolding look.

"I thought something must have happened to you."

"Everything was fine."

"Did you find what you were looking for?"

"I did. Thank you. Do you want me to tell the little girls that it's closing time?"

"What little girls? You're the only visitor we've had all afternoon."

Karen whirled around. The children had been seated at the table when she returned to the desk, now the table was empty. She rubbed her temples. "Perhaps I was mistaken. It's been a long day."

The librarian's features softened. "I hope you'll come back. It gets lonely here. Nobody reads anymore what with television and computers."

"There's still some of us left, Mrs. Hester."

Karen left the old lady to her tsk, tsking.

# Chapter Twenty-Four

She avoided the desk when she entered the hotel and headed straight for the elevator. She needed time to separate fact from fiction. The horror of what her aunt had said would be with her forever, yet the trip to the library had opened a whole new world. Where was the truth? As the elevator crawled its snail-like ascent, she was aware of a presence behind her.

"Hi, Karen, did you forget me?" The voice was bright, inquisitive.

She whirled around and saw the little girl from town.

"You startled me, Anna. I thought I was alone. What are you doing here? I said I'd bring the bracelet back."

"Momma called and said she'd be at the hotel, so I wanted you to meet her."

"And you came all the way here to tell me that?"

"It's not far. How come you look so funny? Don't you want to see her?"

"I'm rather busy at the moment." The elevator wobbled to a stop on the second floor. "Why are we stopping here? There's nothing on this floor."

"This is where momma said to meet her."

"This floor hasn't been used in years." Karen started to push the third floor button but Anna stopped her.

"She said the *second* floor."

"But there's nothing here! The whole floor's empty!"

Anna pushed the 'open' button and Karen saw a brilliantly lit hallway, with fresh flowers meticulously arranged on a table by the wall. A mirror behind the flowers sparkled as if just polished. Surprised, Karen murmured, "They must have just opened the floor."

A man and woman stepped into the elevator, the woman in a purple, ankle-length skirt and boots, her long hair blonde and shiny in a style popular a few years back, the man in black leather as if he had just stepped out of the Pirates of the Caribbean.

The temperature had dropped twenty degrees.

A little boy wearing an E.T. costume ran past chasing a ball. "Tommy Johnson, you come back right now!" shrieked a woman straight out of The Addams Family. "Your daddy's gonna blow his top if you're not ready to go by the time he gets home!" She gave the child a sharp whack on his behind. "You get back in that room or you're not gonna watch The Mouseketeers!" Whining and squirming, the child was marched back into room 202.

"I didn't know the Mouseketeers were still on television," Karen turned to whisper to Anna, but the little girl was nowhere in sight.

Suddenly someone tapped Karen on her shoulder, making her start.

"Boo!" Anna giggled. "Did I scare you?"

Exasperated Karen said, "I told you, I'm busy; I don't have time to play games. Where did you go?"

"I just got water at the fountain."

Karen looked around the hall. "I don't see a fountain. Where's your mother? I thought you wanted me to meet her."

"That's right, in here." Anna opened the door to room 209.

"Don't go in there!" Karen cried, aware of a crunching in her stomach.

"But this is where momma said to meet her. She'll be here in a minute." A weak sun spread faint shafts of light onto the freshly polished furniture in room 209. "What's the matter, Karen? You look funny!"

"How could they have redone this room and the rest of the floor so quickly?"

"What do you mean?"

Karen rubbed her temples. "Something strange is going on; that's all. My head aches. I'm going up to my room."

"Please stay, Karen!" Anna jumped on one of the beds. "Momma will be here soon."

Karen gave in to the child's pleading. "Five minutes, then I really have to go. I'm tired and want to take a nap."

"I like it when we stay here. The beds are so soft."

"Do you come here often?"

"Sometimes, when people visit for Mardi Gras and weddings."

"Is that why your mother is meeting us here? Does she have out-of-town guests?"

"Un-huh," Anna answered drowsily, her voice muffled by a pillow which almost buried her head.

"Anna, I haven't got all day."

"She won't be long. You might as well sit while we wait." The little girl nodded toward the other bed.

Karen sat on the bed. "I'm afraid I can't give your mother more than fifteen minutes, then I'll have to -" The mattress *was* soft, softer than the cement slab in her room. A stupor oozed through her body. She stretched out on the bed, giving way to the downy surface. "This bed must be made of feathers. I can't keep my eyes open."

The little girl laughed. A child's echoing giggle came from across the room. Karen looked over at Anna but her eyes were closed and she seemed to have fallen asleep. There *was* no other child - she and Anna were alone. The room was still, waiting for something to happen.

Then a flurry of giggles started up again, muffled, as if a child were holding her hand over her mouth to keep quiet.

"Did you hear that?" Karen spoke loudly, trying to jolt the child awake.

Anna's eyes popped open. "Did I hear what?"

There was a series of wild bleats - now close to Anna's bed, now close to Karen's. "Can't you hear it?"

"Oh, that's just Odette. Sometimes she sounds like a goat."

"Baaa – baaa" came a faint cry from the cot.

Karen remembered the voodoo doll. "You called her Odette - I knew an Odette -" she said groggily, drifting off. She came awake with a start, "- who stole something of mine. Where is she? I don't see anyone."

"Her mother worked for Momma; don't you remember? She's not supposed to be here. She'll be in *big* trouble."

"There's no one here but us. Are you making those noises, Anna? If so, I'd like you to stop. It's not funny!"

"I'm not doing *anything*."

A jumble of laughter circled the room as if someone were playing hide-and-seek.

Someone - or *thing* - pulled Karen's hair. "Are you playing tricks, Anna? Are you doing that?"

"I'm not doing *anything*, Karen. I *told* you it was Odette. She's fooling around like she always does."

A puff of breath caressed Karen's face as if waiting to see what she would do.

"Look. I don't know what's going on. I'm sorry I missed your mother, but I'm leaving now." Her knees buckled when she tried to walk to the door. A bright orange flare blanketed the walls and she felt searing heat at her back. She blinked and the harsh color was gone. "What was that light? It looked almost like fire."

Anna shrugged and the laughter began again, changing to screams which stopped as quickly as they began. Someone knocked at the door. Karen didn't know who was standing on the other side of the door, but didn't like the person. She felt herself drifting away to another time when she was young and angry all the time.

She turns to the pretty little girl in the pink dress standing next to her. "I bet it's your mama," she says. "What'll I do?"

"Don't you dare tell her we're here," the child whispers back.

The voice on the other side of the door is loud, furious. "Karen, you were a naughty girl to make all that fuss at the wedding! I'm locking you in to punish you."

A key turns in the lock.

"Aunty, no! Please don't lock me in! I promise I'll be good."

A voice laced with fury floats through the door.

"You'll have plenty of time to think about being good. You're going to miss the reception, thanks to your spiteful behavior."

"Please, Aunty?"

"Where's my daughter? Is she in there with you?"

"Say no," the child hisses.

"Are you talking to someone? Is someone in there with you?"

"*No!!! Tell her NO!*"

"No, ma'am," Karen says obediently.

"You better not be lying to me!"

Heels tap down the hall, away from room 209, leaving the two alone. Karen turns to the girl who ordered her to lie, but she's no longer there.

"Who were you talking to, Karen? You were babbling up a storm." Karen rubbed her eyes, wondering why Anna was staring at her so intently. "You were with her today, weren't you? Now you know who my mother is."

"I *don't* know who your mother is, I've never met her," Karen mumbled through a mouth full of mush, her tongue swollen from the strong effect of the pill. Was she making sense? She couldn't tell.

"You *know* who she is," Anna said quietly.

Karen tried to focus on what the child was saying, but she was talking in riddles.

"You talked to her today," Anna persisted. "You found out who you are, didn't you?"

Like a ship looming out of a dense fog, the pieces began to connect.

"You're not real, are you?" Karen slurred the words. "You're dead, aren't you? You died a long time ago."

"Touch me, Karen. See if I'm real."

"No, I won't touch you. Go away. Leave me alone."

Anna began to sing in a high, quivering voice - a song Karen had heard before: "Oh, bad Karen, oh don't you cry for me -"

Karen tried to slap her, to make her stop, but her hand felt nothing but air. She could see and hear Anna, but couldn't feel her. The little girl laughed. "You look so funny, Karen, like you see a ghost."

Using every bit of strength she could gather, Karen swung her feet to the floor, pushed herself off the bed and swayed to the door. She tried to turn the knob, but the door wouldn't open.

"Don't you remember, Karen? She said she was locking the door."

"I don't care what she said, I'm not staying in this room." Karen pounded the door with her fists.

"*And* you're a grouch! I told you momma will be here soon, and she'll let us out, so I don't know why you're all excited. There's nobody here but you and me, and *I* won't hurt you."

Karen looked around the room, empty but for the two of them. But she had heard laughter. She felt she was floating through space. "You mentioned some-one called Odette. Is another child here? If so ask her to stop playing games."

"She'll come out when she's good and ready. It doesn't do any good to yell 'cause nobody can hear us. They couldn't hear us before 'cause they were mak-ing too much noise downstairs." She paused. "I'm glad you call me Anna. I hated it when you called me Joanna."

Someone pushed Karen from behind. She spun around to confront her attacker, but no one was there.

"*That's* Odette," Anna giggled. "Oh, bad Karen, oh, don't you cry for me. We'll tie you up and lock you in; you never will be free," she sang lightly, mocking the menace of the words. The room ricocheted with the laughter of children, seen and unseen.

Karen tried the door again but is unable to open it. She cried out in a thin, frightened voice, "Can anyone hear me? Is anyone there?"

"You don't get it, do you, Karen? I told you; *no one* could hear us back then. That's why it was so great. We could make all the noise we wanted, and no one could hear."

# Chapter Twenty-Five

$\mathcal{L}$ike plowing through a river of molasses, Karen staggered toward the drapes covering the French doors and groped through yards of heavy velvet, scattering ancient dust in the air where it floated in sunbeams as thick as California smog on a summer's day. When she finally uncovered the knotted rope, she pulled triumphantly, only to have the rotted cord break off in her hand.

"Now you've done it," Anna cried.

Sweat dripped from Karen's limp hair; her nose and throat were caked with layers of dust as she tried to ease the drapes along the track. Rusted from years of disuse, the curtain track refused to allow the rings to slide along the rod. She fumbled blindly through the curtain opening until she found a door handle.

Anna quietly watched the silent struggle. "Can't you remember anything, Karen?"

Ignoring her, Karen continued to work at the corroded door catch, wondering in her frustration why hotel owners would allow exits to fall into such disrepair.

"You always were a smart aleck 'cause you thought you were so good," Anna sneered.

"I don't know what you're talking about. Hold these drapes, so I can get the doors open."

"How can I? I'm not here. You said I wasn't real. We're two floors up. What are we supposed to do - jump?"

Karen stopped picking at the latch. "I'll call the manager to let us out." She looked around. No telephone. She swayed on her feet. "This is ridiculous! All hotel rooms have telephones."

"Even if they've been empty for years?"

Walls were closing in.

"Your mother will let us out."

Absurd idea. The mother wouldn't be any more tangible than this small, scarred child that she couldn't touch.

Anna moved to the cot across the room. "You made me sleep here 'cause you couldn't stand to have anybody in bed with you. Remember, Karen?"

Karen stamps her foot. "I can sleep by myself if I want to, so there!" She sticks out her tongue at the whiney little girl.

Anna's voice gets louder "You're so stuck up! You think you're so beautiful! I think you're ugly! So does momma. She told me so."

Karen brushed her hand over her eyes. "Anna, we're still playing games, I want it stopped!"

"Who's playing games? Momma said I could go to Mardi Gras after the reception, but you had to spoil it! I was going to have so much fun in New Orleans! Momma said I could wear my flower-girl dress. Odelia was going to take me and Odette. Then you spoiled everything. I hate you!"

Slipping in and out of reality, overwhelmed by an aching fatigue, Karen lay back on the bed to watch the child storming around the room like a raging queen. Gradually drawn into the morbid performance, she muttered. "I didn't spoil anything. You can still go to Mardi Gras."

Anna continued to spring from wall to wall, her dark hair masking her face like Spanish moss concealing a blemished blossom. "I couldn't go because you were so awful at the wedding! You kept yelling, 'I don't want him to marry her! I hate her! That was so mean, Karen, everyone was mad at you and momma said if you kept that up you couldn't go to Mardi Gras. I was glad 'cause I didn't want you with us anyway. You kept crying like a baby, so she sent you up here. Then the stupid wedding got boring, so me and Odette sneaked up here to play wedding. Remember?" Anna asked savagely.

Karen saw the flicker of orange on the wall again. "I didn't want to play ,but you made me. Said I couldn't go to Mardi Gras if I didn't. You were the bride, and Odette was the groom. I had to be the minister."

Their voices overlapped until it was no longer possible for Karen to tell present from past, reality from fantasy. She sat cross-legged on the bed twisting a strand of her hair as Anna knelt next to her and whispered in her ear, "Then do you remember what you did?"

"No! I didn't do it! Don't tell! Don't tell them I did it!"

"'Member that other time Momma caught you? She was so mad; she walloped the daylights out of you and locked you in the closet but you wouldn't listen. You were so all-fire smart you knew it all, didn't you, Karen?"

"No! You were the smart aleck! You made us play! I didn't want to!"

*The room grows dark, as if a giant black cloud has swallowed up the world.*

*Standing in front of two little girls, Karen is age six again, holding a bible, retrieved from the drawer of the night stand. She is wearing a fluffy pink dress, like a flower girl at a wedding.*

*"If we play wedding, we have to have candles," one of the little girls says, she is very pretty with long dark curls and wears the same kind of dress as Karen.*

*"You not supposed to light matches, girl; Miz Zelena, she say so," Odette, the other little girl says in a frightened voice. She is dark-skinned and her dress isn't as fancy as the other girls'.*

*"She won't know." The girl with the long curls opens the drawer of another nightstand. "Look what I found!" She pulls out two candles and a package of matches.*

*"I'm telling!"*

*"Shut up, Odette! They have candles downstairs; why can't we?" She finds two brass candle holders on the bureau and sticks the tapers in them, then tears a match from the folder and lights one of the candles. "You tell, and you'll get this!" She waves the flickering flame under Odette's turned-up nose, then holds out the candle to Karen. "Hold that while I light the other one."*

*Karen backs away, eyes huge. "No, I won't! Blow it out!" She tries to blow out the flame but the child pulls the candle away from her.*

*"Scaredy cat! Hold that candle or I'll tell momma you were playing with matches and she'll lock you in the closet again."*

*"Don't tell her that! You're the one who lit it, not me!"*

*"Who's she gonna believe? Take it!"*

*Karen nervously takes the candle while the pretty little girl lights the other.*

*"Put them on the nightstands so they'll look like altars."*

*"Oooh, I'm telling," Odette repeats*

*"Will you shut up! You're such a tattle-tale, Odette. Hurry up, Karen, before anyone finds us. You're the minister, marry us!"*

*"This is dumb!"*

*"I'll tell if you don't."*

Scowling, Karen opens the bible. "Do you, Miss Bossy Pants take this nincompoop, Odette Prideux to be your awful wedded chipmunk?"

The girls fall down laughing, getting their party dresses wrinkled and dusty. The girl dressed like Karen has large brown eyes that shine with an innocence not always there. "Finish it!" she cries, getting to her feet. "You're the priest, marry us!"

"I'm not going to play anymore. I won't say it!" Karen pouts, stamping her foot.

"You gotta," Odette says, standing up. "That be what they be saying downstairs."

"Say it!" yells the pretty girl with the curly ringlets. "Say it or I'll tell momma you made us come up here!"

The two girls join hands and dance around Karen singing, "Oh, bad Karen, oh, don't you cry for me. We'll tie you up and lock you in, you never will be free."

She pushes them away. "Okay! Just shut up! I now pronounce you yucky man and stupid wife! Now leave me alone!" She throws the bible on the bed and turns her back on her tormentors.

"Oh, my love, it's been so long," Odette gushes.

"We will go to Vencus and live there forever!" the girl pretending to be the bride croons.

"Stop it!" Karen screams. "You won't go to Vencus! You're not going to live there ever! That's my house just daddy and me live there! You're never going to live there with us!" She pushes the pretend-bride hard, furious at the way the game is going, incensed that this little brat wants to move into her house.

"You quit that!" the other child yells, hurling herself at Karen, missing her, instead knocking over a candle which instantly catches the bedspread on fire. "Put it out! Put it out!" she screams in terror.

Karen grabs the bible from the bed and tries to beat out the flames, but sparks fly on the girl's pink taffeta dress and in seconds it, too, is on fire. Hysterically, the girl on fire dashes around the room thrashing at the flames with her hands, but the faster she runs, the quicker the fire races to her long, twisting curls.

"Help me!" she screams, throwing herself against Odette.

"GET AWAY!" Odette yells thrusting the burning child away.

"I'll get help!" Karen cries and rushes to the door, but it is locked - locked by someone on the other side.

Odette runs to the French doors and pulls back the heavy curtains, but the doors are stuck. After pushing and shoving with all her might she is able to yank one door open and stumble out onto the balcony. Sparks from the bed land on the curtains and they are soon enveloped in flames, trapping the other two children inside the blazing room.

The little girl swathed in flames falls screaming to the floor. Karen tries to run past her, but the pitiful creature grabs her ankle. Karen is backed up against the burning curtains.

"LET ME GO!!!" She shrieks. She kicks herself free and staggers through the fire wall to the balcony where she gasps frantic gulps of fresh air.

A gust of wind, fueled by the raging fire, whips the door from her hands and slams it shut. Almost paralyzed with fear, Karen tries to open the door to free the little girl from the burning room but the door is too heavy, the wind too strong. The last thing she sees is the little girl on her knees, surrounded by flames, feebly banging on the glass door. The right side of her face is melting away.

Karen recoils from the awful sight till she can go no further, trapped by the balcony railing. Her head swerves wildly as she seeks escape. Odette is nowhere to be seen. Could she have jumped to the ground? Karen peers over the railing to the lawn which seems a mile away. Suddenly the French doors shatter with an explosive boom and she has no choice.

She climbs over the balcony rail and eases down the grillwork, dangling precariously, trying to gather courage to jump. Mounting flames urge her on and she drops twenty feet to the lawn below, rolling over and over down the grassy knoll until she comes to a stop on level ground, mere feet from the entrance to the cemetery.

Grateful to find she's still in one piece with only a sharp spasm in her left ankle and blistered hands from the fiery curtains, Karen totters to her feet, anxious to be where it is cool and soothing: the bayou, her refuge when she is lonely and afraid.

She limps through the cemetery, trying not to hear the voices of the dead calling 'Bad Karen!' 'Shame on you!' as she shuffles past their graves. What's that they're chanting? "We'll lock you in and tie you up, you never will be free!" Why are they crying out to her? She did no wrong; she was just trying to save herself.

Prickly vines scratch her arms and legs and tear her dress as she reaches the woods on the outskirts of the graveyard. Soon she will be at the one place that comforted her when her father was away, unable to protect her from her malicious aunt.

She sees the bayou through a clearing and hobbles frantically toward the dark, cool water. In her haste, she fails to see the root of a cypress tree. She trips, and is sent sprawling onto the muddy banks of the bayou.

A full moon shines down on the frantic child who lies motionless, her lungs burning from the fumes of the fire.

She can hear the faraway noise of barking dogs and the even fainter high-pitched whine of sirens. Fire engines? Will they be able to save the pretty little girl in the pink dress? Lights flash through the woods and the dogs get louder.

And then Karen sees the child, her cousin Anna, crawling toward her, screaming, wrapped in flames. She isn't pretty any more. Karen shuts her eyes, praying Anna *won't touch her, won't set her on fire. The screams turn into the shriek of sirens getting closer and closer.*

*When she opens her eyes the girl is gone but Karen can't stop shivering. Was that really Anna, or was Anna's ghost trying to drag Karen back into the flames? Is Anna dead? Or is she still out there in the woods somewhere, trying to find her?*

*A white heron lands on a lily pad, rests a moment, then flies off into the fog.*

*A shadow falls across Karen's face. She is dragged to her feet and shaken violently by a screeching, insane woman: "I'll kill you if you tell anyone who locked that door! Do you hear me? I'll KILL YOU!"*

# Chapter Twenty-Six

*B*o was uneasy. Karen had said she would call after lunch and it was now five o'clock. Soon she'd be leaving for New Orleans. He wanted desperately to see her before she left, to hear what she had learned. He wanted to protect this tough, vulnerable, beautiful young woman who needed him as much as he needed her. He had answered her call, but she hadn't called back. What was going on? He turned to his father who had insisted he join him in a fishing excursion from the pirogue.

"They aren't biting, Papa. I'm going to clean up before I go to the hotel tonight."

"Go on, boy, you ain't got de feel no more since you been at dat damn school."

"It's not that, Papa, the fish are all out partying. I'll catch a table-full tomorrow."

His father threw his line back in. "Tell yo mama to get in mo' tabasco sauce."

After sponging off the smell of bait and putting on a clean shirt and jeans, Bo headed the pickup truck for Vencus.

Karen lay on the bed in her hotel room, sluggish from the drug her aunt had given her. She tried to ignore the furious pounding in her head, but when she opened her eyes and tried to rise from the bed, her head spun more than ever. Fragmented memories overwhelmed her, eclipsed by the sight of a little girl's face on fire. She couldn't concentrate. She needed to get up, but her arms and legs were lead pipes, anchoring her to the bed.

She tried to focus on missing facts the way one would piece together a child's puzzle. The newspaper had printed the news of Richard D'Aquin and *Elena* Benoit's wedding. No mention of Zelena. If the names in the paper were correct, there could only be one conclusion: Richard D'Aquin was her father.

The ghost was gone, couldn't bother her any more. Focus. Nothing made sense. Frustrating to one who could solve a Sudoku puzzle faster than it could be created.

Cool fingers touched her forehead. She flinched from the contact and tried to rise again, but the hands holding her were too strong and she fell back against the pillow.

Someone was speaking: "I'm sorry, Karen, but I must be firm, you're too dizzy to get up. You might hurt yourself."

Who *was* this person? And why would she hurt herself? Did she think she was into self-mutilation?

A face swirled before her. Zelena D'Aquin? Was that her aunt?

"Are you all right?" the woman asked. "You feel feverish."

"I've got to talk to you," Karen said, trying to concentrate on the blurred figure before her. "The library -"

"Oh, yes, Odelia found this in the library." Zelena held out Karen's cell phone. "I knew you'd miss it so I brought it over."

Karen shook her head. That wasn't what she meant; things weren't going the way they were supposed to. "How'd you know I'd be here? This isn't my room."

"The bellboy saw you get in the elevator and it stopped on this floor. He said you looked like you were walking in your sleep." Zelena smiled. 'Like a Zombie' were his exact words. Children are so imaginative. You might have had a bad reaction to my pill. That happens sometimes if you're not used to taking them."

Karen looked around the room. "Where is she?"

"Who?"

"The little girl. Anna."

"Anna?" Zelena looked puzzled. "Who's Anna?"

"She was waiting for her mother."

Karen's headache was becoming unbearable; she shivered and tried not to see flames licking the walls.

"Tell me about Anna."

"I've got to get out of here, I'm supposed to meet someone." Karen fought to get to her feet and lurched for the door, but Zelena blocked her way.

"Not yet," she said softly.

Karen sought the wall for support. "But I have to meet Bo." She looked around at the darkening room. "It's late. What time is it?"

Zelena led Karen back to bed as if she were a child. "You must rest before you go anywhere. You're pale and upset, your friend wouldn't like to see you like this." She touched Karen's temple. "Your pulse is racing a mile a minute. Lie still and you'll feel better." Her steady hand stroked Karen's brow.

A numbness crept through Karen's rigid body. Impossible to move. She strained to hear her aunt's measured words.

"I'm glad you're here. You came to me when I needed comfort, now I can return the favor." Zelena paused. "You saw my daughter, didn't you?"

Karen closed her eyes and shuddered. "I don't think so. I didn't know you had another daughter."

"I only had one. She was so young, with the world before her. Do you remember her? Do you remember Anna?"

Karen tried to stay awake. Through a dim fog she realized her aunt was saying something important. "But your daughter's name was Joanna." Her mind zigzagged between nightmares and the woman beside her.

"She despised the name Joanna. I was wrong to call her by a name she loathed."

Zelena was quiet so long Karen opened her eyes to be sure she was still there. Her aunt was staring at something Karen couldn't see. Her eyes were glazed and her voice grew softer. "Oh, Anna, please come back, I miss you so," she whispered.

Karen spoke through a haze, fighting to straighten out the twisted words. "Anna's not your little girl!" she blurted out. "The child I met - you're not her mother, you can't be." It was hard to stay awake. "The white house - the picket fence -"

"That's where we lived for a while. I'm glad to know it's still there."

Karen leaned on one elbow, unable to sit up, slurring her words. "They're not the same, you know. Your daughter died when she was six; I saw her grave." She had to focus; important things were being said.

Her aunt frowned. "You saw her. You're remembering."

Karen leaned back, struggling to separate reality from nightmare. Images of a fire rushed through her head. Was *that* real? Did the fire really happen? Was that *herself* as a little girl pretending to be a minister? Did they really light those candles?

All at once Karen was on her knees, rocking back and forth on the bed, her voice rising to a child's high pitch. "Yes, I saw her, both of them. Joanna and Odette. I didn't want to play, but they made me!"

Zelena was still a moment, then smiled calmly and handed Karen another pill. "Take this, dear, it's not as potent as the other. You've got to relax. You're terribly distraught. Just swallow it and you'll be fine."

"No!" Karen screamed, spinning back into the present world. "I've got to get out of here!"

She twisted her head back and forth but Zelena pushed her back upon the bed and forced the pill between her lips.

"You want to be ready for tonight, don't you, dear? You need to relax." She stroked Karen's throat as one would entice an unwilling cat.

Puzzled, Karen stared at her aunt; what an odd thing to do. She swallowed, not sure of what would happen if she didn't. She struggled to concentrate on more important things: "The library," she whispered, "- my mother - beautiful wedding -"

Zelena laughed. "Of course my wedding was beautiful - in the beautiful garden of Vencus. And I was the beautiful bride."

Karen stared into the crazed eyes of her aunt. "No, your wedding was here. In this hotel. Downstairs. You locked the door – you thought you were just locking *me* in."

"Did I?" Zelana laughed again. "Perhaps I did." Her laughter became a low, guttural snarl. "But you shut the door in my daughter's face, didn't you? *You* kept her from escaping the terrible fire."

"No! It was the wind! I remember now. The wind blew the door shut."

"Liar. Not the wind - *you*!" Zelena paused a moment then spat out the venomous words: *"Why did you kill my daughter?"*

Karen was astounded at the accusation. "I didn't kill her, Zelena. She grabbed my ankle and wouldn't let go. Her clothes and skin and hair were on fire so I - I guess I pushed her away. I'm sorry - I had to get out!"

Zelena slapped Karen's face. Was she still in the closet where her aunt had locked her so many times before? She couldn't tell, everything was dark, and her head was swirling around and around. "I'm sorry, Aunty" she whimpered, "I didn't mean to hurt Anna."

Zelena seized Karen's hair, twisting her head back till Karen thought her neck would snap. "You didn't just *hurt* her; you *killed* her!"

"Anna's not dead. She's here, waiting for you," Karen gasped, struggling to get away from Zelena's grip.

Her aunt abruptly released her.

"I know she's here. She always is."

And then Karen realized why her mind had closed down all those years ago.

*She* was responsible for the death of her cousin, this woman's only child - Anna - Joanna. She should have pried open the door, pulled her cousin out onto the balcony.

But what would Anna look like today if she had lived?

She knew what Anna would look like.

Like the little girl with the terrible scars who lived in the white house.

The little ghost.

"She has scars," Karen whispered "She must have hurt so badly -"

Zelena struck her in the face, then again and again. The blows were harsh, but Karen didn't defend herself; she must have deserved the violence if she had let Anna die. "There were no scars on my daughter's face until you burned her alive!" her aunt screamed. "She was perfect until you killed her. You are a murderer!"

Zelena abruptly released Karen and took a lighter from her purse. She flicked it until a steady flame appeared, then held the tiny flame to the bed-spread as casually as if she were lighting a cigarette. "I wonder if *you'll* live to have scars like Joanna."

The flame spread quickly, the material being old and dry.

Then Zelena set the drapes on fire.

Karen watched as if seeing an old movie on television, her brain as limp as her body.

Her aunt left the blazing room as quietly as she had entered.

As the fire crept closer, Karen wondered how soon the pain would begin. The drapes would take longer to burn than the bedspread, she reasoned, since the material was heavier. She became fascinated by the design the flames made as they spiraled slowly upward across the crest of the drapes. Pretty, very pretty. Flying sparks reminded her of Fourth of July celebrations at the beach in Santa Monica. They arced brilliantly, then scattered haphazardly to the floor. She wondered how long it would take the thick rug to catch fire - longer than the drapes, she mused.

A series of rings near her ear became louder, more insistent the longer they rang. She frowned as she wondered where the noise was coming from. It was annoying, made her headache worse. A little black box by her side was beeping, demanding her attention. She tried to shake it, make it stop, but her fingers wouldn't close around it properly, so she knocked the buzzing to the floor.

Someone was calling her name from far away. "Karen! Karen, are you there?" She giggled. Well, of course she was here, where else would she be? The voice went on and on: "Why don't you answer? Are you all right? Call me!" She laughed at the idea of someone on the floor yelling "Call me." She looked at her legs, and the same funny orange pattern that was on the drapes began to crawl up her clothes.

Suddenly, she was afraid. How could Anna have stood the pain? She tried to beat out the flames with her hands but she had no strength and the fire was burning too fast. Panic took over and the need for survival pulled her to her feet. She was *not* going to die in this room like Anna. She walked unsteadily to the door that led to the hall, avoiding patches of fire around her. She twisted the searing hot knob but the door was locked as it had been before. Locked from the outside.

Whispers came from behind her - a child's whisper by the burning bed. "You saw her, didn't you, Karen?"

Karen spun around. "Anna! Where did you go?"

"I was here. I'm always here. I can't leave, not anymore."

Her scars were gone and she was dressed in a pink, taffeta dress soon to be ashes. She was a ghost, a baby ghost. Karen saw through her to the burning drapes. The little ghost sang sadly, eerily: "Oh, bad Karen, oh, don't you cry for me. I'll tie you up, and lock you in. You never will be free."

"No! You can't keep me here; you're not real." Whispers circled around her as she edged closer to the French doors, her only exit.

"Stay with me, Karen," Anna begged. "Don't leave me again."

Dream, specter, the subconscious, whatever Anna was, Karen had to save herself or soon she would be the same as the child - nothing more than a wisp of smoke.

She dragged a chair to the doors and with a strength she wasn't aware of, smashed the glass, fracturing it into a thousand fragments. Gulping fresh air, she stepped out onto the safety of the balcony.

She looked back into the burning room and saw Anna for the last time, her face a hideous mass of scars.

# Chapter Twenty-Seven

Karen climbed over the iron railings surrounding the balcony and saw the oblique lawn below - a far drop, but one she had survived before. Flames raced along the wooden planks of the balcony. Let me live, she prayed to a God she hadn't spoken to for a long time, then fell to the rolling grass below. Surprised that she was unhurt when she landed, merely badly jolted, she gave thanks to that same God, then scrambled to her feet and started running, knowing somewhere she would soon be safe.

She came to the gates of the cemetery. Could her cousin with the burning face find her here? She ran on, trying to shut out voices from the past. "This way, Karen!" "Hide and seek, Karen, just like old times!" "Don't let the ghosts get you, Karen!"

She reached the end of the cemetery and came to a copse of dense shrubs and towering trees. Somewhere through that jungle she had once found peace. She ran past grasping vines trying to trap her and failed to see the roots of a twisted cypress tree protruding from the ground. She sprawled on moist soil, yet welcomed the coolness of the marshland beneath her body, the dark waters of the swamp almost within reach.

"Good evening," Bo said politely to the woman standing before him. "I'm looking for my friend Karen Benoit. She was meeting her aunt earlier for lunch. Can you tell me if she's still here?" He waited patiently for an invitation to step inside, but the sour-faced woman merely grunted and slammed the door in his face. Karen was right, the housekeeper was a harridan.

Wondering what the hell was going on, Bo waited in the dark for another two minutes before knocking again. He could see lights throughout the impressive estate. Apparently no one inside was willing to accept intruders. A final explosive brass knocker pounding, loud enough to wake the entire population of Bayou Vieux Cemetery, brought results - the sound of shuffling feet approaching the door. Bo squelched his anger as the door slowly opened - pointless to show rage. The dim light revealed a stooped, reedy, silver-haired man; the sometime Voodoo Queen lurked in the shadows behind him.

Bo spoke into the semi-darkness, "Good evening Sir, I'm looking for your niece, Karen Benoit. I believe she was here earlier."

The older man spoke curtly over his shoulder. "Odelia, get Mrs. D'Aquin. She can clear this up for the gentleman."

"She not be here."

"Well, where is she?" Bo heard alarm in D'Aquin's voice. "Someone wants to see her!"

"Actually I'm looking for -" Bo started to say, but was cut short by the brusque housekeeper.

"She be with dogs. She walking dem."

D'Aquin voice shook and the veins in his forehead jumped as if triggered by a switch. "I *told* you not to let her go out! Especially with those damn dogs. She's not well!"

"Miz D'Aquin, she go where she please." Odelia said calmly, then added maliciously, "She be wear dat same white dress she always wear. She say it her wedding dress."

Tension simmered as the two glared at each other, D'Aquin almost apoplectic, Odelia stoic as a Greek stature. A distant sound of sirens halted the mounting battle as the three turned in unison toward the source of the noise.

A red glow had settled in the sky near the St. Francis Hotel.

"My God, the hotel is on fire!" D'Aquin cried. Frowning, he turned back to Odelia, "Did Zelena say she was going over there? Answer me! Where was she going?"

"She say nothin', she just go."

Bo had already started for the truck.

"Wait!" D'Aquin shouted. "I'm going with you."

Bo's mind spun with uncertainty as he raced his truck toward the hotel with Karen's uncle slumped at his side, mumbling to himself. Keeping an eye on the twisting road Bo shouted in the old man's ear, "What the hell's going on? Where is Karen?"

"I should have stopped it when I could," the old man muttered vaguely.

"What are you talking about?" Bo shook the old man with his free hand, but D'Aquin slipped further down in his seat refusing, or unable, to answer.

The hotel grounds were chaotic. Half-costumed mummies and cat women were streaming onto the wide lawn loudly protesting they had balls or parades to attend and hotels shouldn't be allowed to catch fire. Bo spotted Lou lounging on the lawn and yelled "What happened? What caused the fire?"

"Beats me. It started on the second floor. Probably faulty wires. This damn hotel - hey, where you going," Lou hollered as Bo sprinted for the entrance. "You can't go in there, they made us all get out!"

"I'm looking for" Bo began, then stopped as he saw D'Aquin crumple to the ground, still babbling. Bo eased the older man to a sitting position, relieved to see his color slowly returning and his breathing almost normal. "Take care of him, will you, Lou? Call an ambulance, he might be in shock. I've got to find Karen!"

Without waiting for a reply, Bo pushed his way into the hotel only to be blocked by hysterical, half-dressed guests being herded through revolving doors.

Escaping the mob, Bo rushed to the stairway where a harassed-looking fireman barred his way. "No way, buddy, this place is being evacuated."

"I'm looking for my girl. She may be upstairs."

"If she is, they'll get her, don't worry."

"Not good enough, I'm going up." He dodged past the fireman and took the stairs two at a time.

Two firefighters were splintering the door when he arrived at 209. "What are you doing here?" one of the burly men yelled at Bo. "Get back downstairs!"

"I'm a doctor!" Bo shouted, embellishing his recent graduation. "They told me to come up here."

The man shrugged, then turned back to the final demolition of the door. As it crashed to the floor a cloud of black smoke enveloped the three men. Coughing and choking, Bo burst into the room in time to see a powerful stream of water spurt through the open balcony and flood the room, soaking what seconds ago had resembled the insides of a furnace. Bo covered his nose to ward off the acrid stench of smoldering wood: black, charred furniture ready to crumble at a touch.

The room was empty.

"Looks like we don't need you, Doc. Better go see what you can do downstairs."

Bo clattered back downstairs, frantic to get further information from Karen's uncle.

Dazed and unsure of himself. D'Aquin sat on a fussy white, wrought-iron bench that added to the Civil War look of the old hotel. Lou hovered near by, unwisely smoking a cigarette. "I called an ambulance," he scoffed in a tone that implied hell would freeze over before one would come. "This town isn't exactly NYC when it comes to services. The whole place is an uproar with *that* going on." He nodded at the milling crowd. Hostility hung in the air like a cloud of angry mosquitoes. "How's the old guy? Can he talk?"

"Maybe had a small stroke. He's talking but not making much sense. I wouldn't get him riled, might make it worse. Ambulance should be here soon. He'll have to go to Lafayette."

Bo crouched next to the old man. "Remember me, Mr. D'Aquin? Bo Boudreau, I drove you here. How're you feeling?"

D'Aquin looked up from the study of his hands. "You find them?" His eyes lost focus and he went back to bantering jokes with cronies only he could see. Once in a while he'd switch to a dialogue with himself. Bo leaned closer to make sense of the rambling. "Zelena - Karen - poor little Karen - where'd she go? Never could find that poor child."

"Yes, Karen. I'm trying to find her. Do you know where she is? She hasn't been in Bayou Vieux long enough to know her way around."

"Loves bayou - hides - Zelena hates - should have stopped - too late...." D'Aquin's head dropped to his chest, tears streaking down his cheeks.

Bo sprang to his feet. "Stay with him, Lou. I have to find Karen."

Time was meaningless as Karen lay on the muddy ground, listening to creatures of the bayou. Above the hoot of an owl, the chatter of hidden birds, frogs, night animals, she heard a high-pitched whine reminding her of - what? She was glad when the noise stopped; it had disturbed her secret world.

Another sound invaded her senses, thrashing and thumping as bushes were trampled. The panting and wheezing grew closer. A beast, anxious to find its prey? Harsh growls, the sound of snuffling turned urgent. Suddenly Odin and Zeus burst through the thicket into the clearing, headed straight for her, Odin in the lead, the blind one behind, sniffing the ground, as sure of his goal as was his leader. Zeus she wasn't afraid of - they had bonded only hours before

- but the Mastiff was terrifying; she had felt his hot breath on her face. She reeled to her feet, gathering sticks, rocks - anything for protection.

She was shocked to see who followed them.

"Get back here, you miserable mutts!" Zelena in torn, white rags swirling about her as she stumbled into the clearing, face pale as the clothes she wore, thick black hair in wild disarray; eyes ebony coals, once carefully applied makeup streaked and smudged on a face ravaged by years of madness, more of a ghost than the child who haunted Karen's dreams.

She snapped the riding crop across the backs of the animals. "*STAY,* black devils!" Whimpering, the dogs sprawled at her feet.

Zelena turned to Karen, cracking her whip in the air. "Why are you here? Why didn't you burn to death like my daughter? *How dare you be alive?*"

Groggy but inflamed by the insane ranting Karen cried, "You drugged and tried to kill me! You meant to burn me alive!"

"Yes! Like you did to my precious baby!" Zelena spat out the words.

"I was *six-years-old, Zelena!* The wind slammed the door shut! In that room before you came - I saw it happen! I remembered everything!"

"Because of *her!* She came to you as she comes to me every night. *Crying!* Because she'll never have the life you have. Night after night I see her!"

Zelena doubled over with grief, her misery reaching out to Karen in a way anger never could.

Karen's voice softened. "That's why you asked me to come here. You wanted revenge for something I never did."

"*Liar!*"

"I trusted you, I thought I'd find out the truth but instead I was served a packet of lies. I know now that Richard D'Aquin isn't my uncle - he's my father!"

"*No!*"

"How did you get him to lie for you, Zelena? How did you turn him into a zombie?"

"You're the liar!" Zelena screamed, and lashed the crop across Karen's face in a hysterical rage.

Caught off guard, Karen fell to the ground, the whip slashing at arms and body already raw from the devastating fire. Memories of other locked rooms, whippings by a violent, out of control woman brought her to her feet again and she knew that only force would overcome the wrathful lunatic before her.

"No!" she shouted, "you can't do this to me; I won't let you!" Yanking the whip from her aunt's clenched fists, Karen hurled it into the swamp. "It's *your* fault Anna died! If you hadn't locked that door, she'd be alive today. You *know* that!" Frightened by her own anger, Karen wheeled around and tried to walk away from the old woman.

"You will *not* get away this time!" Zelena screeched, clawing at Karen's throat. The attack threw the girl off balance and they fell awkwardly down the bank to the water's edge, Zelena clinging to Karen like a rabid dog savaging his prey. The two women thrashed about in the murky water, slipping in slime-filled pot holes. Zelena shrieked like a wounded animal and staggered to her feet, still trying to squeeze the life out of her hapless niece. Karen fought to escape, yet was unwilling to hurt someone whose mind had reached that level of insanity where revenge was the only answer to years of frustration and hatred.

Youth won out as Karen was finally able to pry Zelena's bony fingers from her neck and thrust her back into the murky water. Her aunt was, in spite of her frenzy, a feeble woman; surprise was her ally, her only real strength.

Breathing heavily, Karen hunched over in the shallow water, took a deep breath and regarded her aunt sprawled in an undignified clump in the bog. "You're sick, Zelena. Come, I'll take you back and we'll get help for you."

Zelena rose shakily from the water, her gown filthy from sludge and muck. "I don't want your help! You're the devil! Odin! Zeus! *Attack!*"

Up to now the dogs had remained motionless on their bellies, but now, responding to Zelena's violent commands, they lurched to their feet and waded into the water, uttering low growls. Karen moved into deeper water, away from the dogs. "Call them off, Zelena! I never hurt you."

"You ruined my life!" the crazed woman shouted,

Zelena grabbed the floating crop from the still water and began flailing the nearest dog, Odin, the dangerous one. "Get her, you stupid hound! *KILL HER!*" She battered the dog about his head, cursing, urging him to attack Karen. Enraged by the beatings, the animal turned on his mistress, snarling furiously.

"Stop hitting him, Zelena!" Karen cried. "He's savage!"

"He won't hurt me; he's mine! He always obeys me!" The lashes continued. "Attack *her*, *idiot*, not me! I own you! You'll do what I say!"

Odin's throat rumbled fiercely as he stalked his mistress, source of perpetual brutal beatings.

"Monster!" Zelena screamed, backing away from the slowly advancing dog. "Keep away, you stupid beast!"

Odin lunged at her.

Stunned by the attack, Zelena lost her balance and fell backward again into the swamp, dropping the whip as she fell. Karen struggled to reach her, but was blocked by Zeus who furiously joined the assault. As Zelena tried frantically to ward off the dogs, a dark shadow moved swiftly through the water toward them.

"Zelena!" Karen cried. "Behind you! Get up!" She looked around for rocks, sticks, anything to throw at the creature who was bearing down on the frenzied woman. Karen tried to wade through the murky waters to reach her aunt before the alligator attacked, but she was too far away. She called again, *"Zelena, look out!"*

Zelena glanced over her shoulder in time to see gaping, enormous jaws inches from her face. *"NO!"* she screamed. *"Tainted Kietre! No! Go away!"* Paralyzed with fear, she watched in horror as the creature sank its teeth into her arm. White lilies turned crimson from Zelena's blood.

Karen struggled through the dense water toward her aunt. The crop floating by her aunt's side was within easy reach; she plucked it from the water and with all her might brought it down on the beast's snout. Stunned, the creature released its prey and turned on the aggressor. Odin and Zeus advanced toward the beast, yowling non-stop, their snarling jaws and fangs glistening in the moon's rays. As the animal bore down on Karen, Zeus clamped razor-sharp teeth on the creature's tail while Karen thrashed its head, snout and eyes with the whip.

Confused by the challenge, the sting of the whip, the aggressive assault on its tail, the beast paused as if to reconsider the prudence of attack; the chase was no longer worthwhile. It turned, flicking Zeus away with his tail as if the dog was no bigger than a yappy terrier, then moved unhurriedly through the dark waters of the bayou, away from the exhausted combatants.

Was the alligator 'Gonfle', Tank's 'friendly' denizen of the bayou, too lazy to continue his search for dinner, 'Tainted Kietre', the supernatural bog-dweller feared by the locals of Bayou Vieux, or did Karen and the dogs really drive away a dangerous predator who could easily have eaten them alive? The trio watched anxiously as the black shadow silently retreated into darker waters. Seeing they were no longer in danger, Karen turned to her aunt, half in, half out of the stagnant water. Bleeding had stopped, cauterized by the cold mud that almost buried Zelena's arm, but her skin was as white as the water lilies had been, now tinted by the dying woman's blood. She shivered uncontrollably.

Like a balloon losing air, Karen felt herself drained of the energy that had pitted her against the alligator, and she slipped to her knees next to Zelena. With one last effort she flung her arm over her aunt, trying to keep her warm.

Odin raised his massive head and howled, then circled the two women as if warding off creatures of the night. Zeus nudged Zelena once, trying to urge life into her, then joined Odin in his mournful vigil.

The two women lay still as corpses on the bank of the bayou - one half dead, and the other perhaps already in that state of nirvana.

# Chapter Twenty-Eight

Having spent his whole life on the bayou, Bo was totally familiar with the swamps of Louisiana, but the bayou that stretched from Vencus to the Bayou Vieux Cemetery had more twists and turns than a roller coaster, and he knew the small inlets and recesses could provide dozens of hiding places for a frightened child. Would Karen remember the secret passages she once sought, or was that knowledge also lost in time? If her uncle made any sense in his ramblings, she would be somewhere along the bayou, with or without her aunt. He didn't know how the hotel fire had started, but from what Karen had told him of the old lady, Zelena, no doubt, had something to do with it.

His path began at the edge of the cemetery, just beyond the hotel, and the musky smell of fetid waters steered him through tangled brush and decaying vegetation. He was thankful he had brought a flashlight; no one wanders the thickets of a Louisiana swamp at night without one. Enchanting during the day, Bayou Vieux was fearful when the sky turned black. He scanned the treetops with the light, watchful for snakes. It would take only one bite from a water moccasin to send him to the hospital, and he silently prayed Karen wouldn't come in contact with one of the poisonous vipers.

Suddenly he heard the deep-throated howl of a dog, followed by another, less aggressive wail. Zelena's dogs? He pushed through the fortress of vines till he came to a clearing, just at the water's edge. The hounds turned on him, their doleful wailing shifting to menacing growls as they slunk toward him, ready to fight off any intruder who might threaten their wards.

"No, Zeus, Odin, stay." The weak command alerted the beasts and, uncertain of their duties, they looked in the direction of the voice.

At first Bo failed to see the two bodies huddled together at the water's edge, but when he heard Karen's voice he ignored the pacing dogs and rushed to her side. Almost weeping with relief he pried her away from the lifeless woman's body.

"Thank God, I found you, darling," he cried, lifting her gently in his arms.

"What took you so long, Cherie?" she murmured, snuggling into his warm, protective arms.

He kissed her mud-splotched face and whispered, "You're safe now, ma petite, I'll take you home."

She struggled to break loose. "No - Zelena's hurt. We can't leave her here - we must take care of her!"

"Karen - I don't know what happened, but your aunt is dead. I'm sorry. I'll come back for her."

Sobbing, Karen broke free from Bo and slid to the ground. "No! I'm not leaving her alone out here!" She wrapped her arms around the dead woman's body and tried to lift her. "She'll come with us!"

"I can't carry you both -"

"You don't have to, I'll walk. Zeus will help, won't you, boy?" The dog whimpered and leaned against her, almost knocking her over. She laughed shakily and put her arms around his thick neck. "See? The blind leading the blind. Odin?" She reached out and gently stroked the trembling monster who had swerved to her other side, seeking direction from someone he knew wouldn't hurt him. "You'll help us back, won't you, Odin? Please, Bo, we'll manage. We'll have to, I'm not leaving her."

Bo paused, realizing he had no choice, then gathered Zelena in his arms.

They made a strange procession as they worked their way back to the hotel, Bo stumbling under the weight of the stiffening body, Karen half dragged by the docile animals on either side of her.

Karen stood in the doorway of the hospital room where her father lay, eyes closed. Did he hate her? she wondered. They hadn't seen or spoken to each other since Zelena's death. Did he blame her for that too? She couldn't leave without hearing what he had to say - if he was capable of telling the truth.

As if sensing her presence his eyes flew open and they stared at each other, silently assessing one another. She knew that he was ready for release after the slight stroke and was going back to an empty castle. One of Bo's sisters was staying at Vencus until another housekeeper could be found. Odelia and Odette were gone, having fled to New Orleans, probably causing as much trouble there as in Bayou Vieux.

"Will you sit beside me, Karen?" he spoke at last, his voice quivery, but audible.

"I can't stay long; my plane leaves this afternoon."

"I had hoped you would stay."

"I may be back," she said cautiously.

"You were with Zelena when she died."

"Yes."

"I hope it wasn't too dreadful for you."

"It - wasn't pleasant."

"Her insanity made her a terrible person."

Karen looked surprised. That wasn't what she expected to hear.

"I must tell you the truth. Who you are, who Zelena was, who your mother was."

"I know most of it. You're my father. You married my mother in a lovely ceremony at Vencus."

He closed his eyes. "I'm sorry, Karen. It was unforgivable of me to deceive you, but I just didn't know what to do. I was afraid of what might happen if -"

He was silent a moment. Finally, Karen asked, "Did you ever really love my mother?"

She was pained to see the sorrow in his eyes.

"Oh, yes, Karen. Your mother was a beautiful bride whom I dearly loved."

"What about Zelena?"

He was quite for a long time. "You must forgive me, Karen, your aunt was a desperate woman, coming from New Orleans with a new baby -"

"So the roles were reversed."

"What?"

"Nothing. Go on."

"Your mother was kind to her, took her in in spite of what she had become – there were terrible rumors about Zelana's life in New Orleans."

"I know some of that," she paused, determined to know the rest of the story, "only Zelena told me it was my mother who was the prostitute."

He said nothing, only closed his eyes again as if to block out further proof of Zelena's madness. Perhaps she had said too much. She held her breath, fearful her words would cause another stroke to this new found father of hers. In spite of her anger she wanted so much to love and be loved in return.

At last he spoke. "Apparently her viciousness knew no bound. In the beginning I was deceived, grateful for her help with your mother. We put Zelena in a little cottage in town with her baby. Joanna. Her friend - Odelia - stayed with us at Vencus to take care of your mother who was very sick during pregnancy -"

"- with me."

"With you," He ventured a weak smile. "Then - then - your mother -" He stopped, unable to go on.

"She died, bearing me. I realize that now. Then what happened?"

"This is the hardest part for me to talk about."

"I believe I can fill in the pieces. Zelena was a great consoler. She was ready - eager - to take my mother's place."

"She was a seductress, a witch!" he said harshly. "And I, ever the gullible fool, let her beguile me." His voice broke, and Karen was moved to see tears in her father's eyes. "She treated you badly, Karen, but I was bewitched, pretended not to see. We were married in a small ceremony at the hotel - then there was the terrible fire just as we were saying our vows." He was quiet for a long while, then shook his head, as if suddenly aware of Karen standing before him, waiting for the rest of the story. "Zelina blamed you. Her hatred was unreasonable, but she convinced me to put you up for adoption. I was a coward, unable to stand up to her vicious attacks, so I gave in. Can you forgive me? Is it possible?"

Karen abruptly stood. "I have to go. I'm glad you're well." She left the room quickly, before she collapsed in front of the man she wanted to hate, but couldn't.

# Chapter Twenty-Nine

The red sign blinked repeatedly, warning passengers to fasten their seat belts. Karen give up trying to read and slipped her book into her backpack. She stared out at the solid mass of grey clouds surrounding the plane; they would be landing in fifteen minutes, right on schedule.

Chaotic thoughts swam through her head like mechanical soldiers tumbling over each other. "Let your thoughts flow," the therapist had said. "Don't bury them. Buried hurts must be allowed to surface and be examined. Then, and only then, can you come to terms with yourself and those around you. Your mind must become as healthy as your body is now."

She steeled herself for the wheel's bumpy touchdown and took a deep breath before looking out at the lush green fields surrounding the New Orleans airport. She yearned to revisit the swamp she saw that first day in Louisiana, to see again a snowy white heron gracefully rise from the murky waters of the swamp. Would she be able to see that lovely sight again without seeing her cousin's tortured face?

She'd soon find out.

The impatient flow of passengers leaving the plane herded Karen in automatic step with the crowd. From a distance, she saw Bo's tall, straight back and the trim white hair of the man next to him. She had wanted to be alone with Bo, but now she was forced to confront the other man who seldom left her thoughts. Okay, get it over with; you wanted family, well, you've got it now. She pushed her way through the congestion of travelers and greeters. "Bo! Richard!" she called. "Over here!"

Seated in Bo's weathered compact car, Karen closed her eyes and relived the impact of Bo's lips on hers, the pressure of his arms around her as thrilling as she had remembered. She couldn't wait to be alone with him. He had written a flowery proposal of marriage and she had shot back, '*YES!*' Corky was already picking out her maid-of-honor dress.

Her father spoke from the back seat. "Karen, I'm so happy you're here. I swear I'll do everything possible to compensate for what I did." He cleared his throat. "Everything will be all right, you'll see."

"Sure - Dad." She wondered if he knew what an effort it was to say that word. She concentrated on the lush greenery rolling past her window.

"Does it look the same?" he asked, breaking into her thoughts.

"Greener." Was this proper father-daughter speak?

"Vencus is beautiful now. It put out a burst of color, just for you."

"I can't wait to see it again, Dad." Not so hard this time.

"Karen -" he began, then stopped.

"Yes?" Come on, let's get this touchy-feely part over with.

"I didn't tell you, because, well, I didn't want to disturb you more than necessary." He paused. "And I was a coward."

"I'm okay. No scars."

"You're beautiful, Karen, you always were. It breaks my heart that I never -"

"It's over. In the past. New page, new book."

"Yes, of course." He laughed nervously. "As you say, it's all in the past, darling."

Had he called Zelena darling, too? And her mother? Don't go there. New page, remember?

"Odelia no longer works for me. I let her go after the - accident."

"I know, you told me." She was quiet as they drove past giant oaks that bordered the bayou. "Do you have enough help? Vencus is big."

"The others are still there, Addy, Jerome. I have a new housekeeper, Madeline. I think you'll like her."

"I'm sure I will." The vines were thicker; in places they threatened to strangle the magnolia trees, the oaks, the lush camellia trees. Where did the cypresses begin? The marshes? She strained to see glimpses of dainty egrets. Was that a heron? "And Odette? Is she still around?"

Her father wiped his brow with an immaculately white handkerchief. Nerves? Heat? Stress? She had to be careful; she didn't want to be responsible for any more deaths.

"You okay, Dad?"

"It's getting warm. You'll miss your California breezes."

"Not really."

"You asked about Odette. She and Odelia went back to New Orleans. I don't know what they're doing there. Do you remember Odette as a child?"

"Bits and pieces," she lied. "I ran into her at the hotel."

"She was always under her mother's thumb."

Bo interrupted for the first time. "Last I heard they were doing a brisk voodoo business on Bourbon Street."

She glanced at her father in the mirror. His scowl spoke volumes. Bo should have been more cautious. She spoke louder than intended. "Zeus? Oden? Are they still at Vencus? I hope nobody decided to do anything dire about them. They're good dogs." She had thought about the dogs a great deal; life had not been easy for them. In the end they had saved her life.

Bo smiled. "You don't know Louisiana, dahlin'. We love our dogs. All they needed was a little TLC and now they're doing fine."

"Where?"

"They're with a damn good Cajun family. The Boudreaus,"

"I couldn't handle them, Karen. Bo was kind enough to take them in."

"Always, the rescuer," she said softly.

"Like you say, Cherie, they're good dogs. Once you get used to them you'll love them."

"I already do. Thanks for coming, Dad. I guess we're driving you back to -" she took a deep breath – "Vencus."

"Yes, but aren't you staying with me?"

She looked to Bo for support.

"Karen's staying at my house until things get settled. We have an extra room now that my brother Henri's got an oil rig job in northern Louisiana."

"I see. Sometimes I rattle around in the old place. I might put it on the market."

"You don't want to do that."

"No, I don't."

Karen got a sick feeling in the pit of her stomach as Bo turned into the curving driveway of Vencus. No more ghosts, all in her mind the therapist had said. And yet -

"Won't you even come in and have a drink? Maybe stay for dinner?"

"'Fraid not, Mr. D'Aquin," Bo answered for Karen. "Mama's got a pot of jambalaya waiting for us." He paused. "Maybe you'd like to join us?"

Richard D'Aquin slowly got out of the car. "Oh, I'm sure Madeline's got something on the stove. She's a pretty good cook." Odelia's expertise in the kitchen hung in the air between the three. "Well, we'll be in touch. Please come dine one night – when you're ready," he added quickly.

Wordlessly, Karen and Bo watched the old man shuffle up the stairs into the mausoleum that had been in his family for almost three centuries. After the door closed they were silent while Bo drove back onto Loop Road, each in their own thoughts. Karen broke the silence.

"I'd like you to drive me to 370 Ashcroft, Bo."

"Cherie, there's nothing there, just that old playhouse. I checked after you told me about your - experience."

"I have to see it."

He hesitated. "It's getting dark; you'll need a flashlight."

She opened the glove compartment. "Voila!"

Neither spoke till they came to the near-empty lot, stripped bare but for the neglected playhouse, bruised by years, that Karen had come upon when she was looking for the little white house with the picket fence.

Bo parked the car. "I'll go in with you."

"No, I won't be long."

She noted the large pecan tree as she walked up to the dilapidated shack, ready to fall to the ground, and wondered how long it had been since anyone had picked pecans. The white house had been demolished years ago with still no buyers to build on the weedy lot.

She flicked on the flashlight and ducked low to enter the small building. Smelly and stuffy were her first thoughts, then she caught her breath as she stared at a small table and two chairs occupied by a pair of dressed-up dolls covered in cobwebs and dust. A plate of something resembling rock-hard cookies was set before the silent pair, along with a pitcher and two glasses. Lemonade poured fifteen years earlier? She shivered and waved the flashlight around the walls of the little house. A terrible fear like those which had overpowered her so many times in Bayou Vieux clawed at her gut as she gazed in amazement at the torn, stained wallpaper that still survived in the miniature dining room. Horse-drawn carriages paraded across pale green walls just as she had seen a month ago when a small, scarred little ghost served her lemonade and cookies.

Did she need further proof?

She stifled a scream, almost dropping her flashlight, as something small and quick scurried across her feet.

"You okay, hon?" Bo hovered anxiously outside the playhouse as Karen hastily escaped the oppressive room.

"I'm fine, just one more minute, then we can go."

She fumbled with the catch of the tiny bracelet that had cramped her wrist since Anna had given it to her. She had never taken it off and used to finger it repeatedly as if the small gold chain had answers. Her fingers trembled too much to undo the clasp. She held up her wrist to Bo. "Will you help me take this off, Bo? I'm all thumbs."

"Sure, hold the flashlight." He bent over her arm and, after a brief struggle, undid the clasp and handed her the bracelet. "I know you have a small wrist, but next time get a larger size. Maybe I'll get you one for your birthday."

"Then you see it. The bracelet is there."

"Of course it's there, why wouldn't it -" He glanced at her quickly then looked away, not meaning to question.

She walked back along the weed-filled yard and dropped the bracelet in a spot which once hosted tulips and ranunculus.

Anna would want it back.

They drove in silence pass the cemetery - they didn't have to stop there, she already knew what was in it. Maybe later she would visit the library, the soda shop, the orphanage - all the stops on her last trip. Perhaps she would even visit cheerful, scatterbrained Nurse Lehman and her houseful of cats.

She stared out the window as they approached the St. Francis Hotel; Bo's arm tight around her shoulder. She studied his strong profile which had so often banished nightmares. "With you beside me I think I could spend the night at the St. Francis and not be bothered anymore," she whispered in his ear.

Bo laughed. "We're not spending our honeymoon in that damn hotel if that's what you're thinking!"

"I know, but stop the car in front of it, will you, please? I made a promise to myself a while back, and if I don't do it now I'm afraid I never will."

"Are you sure this is the right time?"

"There can't be a later date. As you and my silly therapist always say: 'Face your fears!'"

Bo gently rubbed her cheek. "No more fears, Karen, I promise." He parked the car and she stepped out. "But this time I *am* going in with you."

"Again, no. Sorry, Bo." She stroked his wonderfully concerned face. "This is a private date."

She looked up at the building. The second floor hadn't changed in the short time she had seen it last, the drapes to other rooms still tightly drawn, 209 boarded up. The wooden planks for windows looked eerie, desolate, even more so than before.

Inside, the same dreary furniture dressed the lobby, empty but for an elderly couple nodding sleepily in armchairs. She smiled upon seeing Telemaque's white head bent over his eternal game of solitaire and tapped him lightly on the shoulder so as not to startle him. "Hi, Tel," she spoke softly. "Remember me?"

The old man looked blankly at Karen before breaking into an enormous smile.

"Oh, Lord, Miz Benoit, you be back!" He pumped her hand vigorously while his eyes filled with tears. "God, almighty, it be good to see you. You look prettier den ever. Do Bo Boudreau know you be back?"

"He's waiting in the car. You feeling okay, Tel? No more flu or whatever plagued you?"

Tel frowned. "It be plague all right, Miz Benoit. We already know what it be." He stared hard at Karen. "Why you be at the St. Francis, Miss? Dis ain't no place for you to be coming to."

"I wanted to say hello to you and Tank. Is he around?"

Telemaque struck the desk bell with his fist. "Yeah, dat lazy grandson of mine, he be around somewhere. Probably shooting craps out in de back with dem other loafers He gran'mere gonna whip he hide, she find out!" He slammed the bell again. "Tank! Get youself in here, boy!"

Kitchen doors banged open and the skinny bellboy galloped toward the desk, jerking up too-large pants as he ran.

"I be helping move some boxes for de cook!" Tank protested, then skidded to a stop when he saw who the visitor was. "Miz Karen!" he yelled, tumbling into her outstretched arms. "Oh, boy, ma'am, you come home!" They hugged for a moment then, afraid of acting the baby, he squirmed out of Karen's arms. "It sure be nice to see you, ma'am," he mumbled, straightening his clothes in embarrassment.

"It's good to see you again, Tank. I think you've grown a foot in a month."

"Me, I be almost twelve now, ma'am," the boy said proudly.

"Me and Tank, we be sorry about Miz D'Aquin -" Telemaque began shyly, then stopped, unsure how to finish.

"I'll give my father your sympathy, Tel, he'll appreciate it." She held out her hand. "If you'll give me the key to room 209 I'd like to go upstairs for a moment."

The old man and the young boy gazed at each other in horror. Tank was the first to recover. "No way, Miz Karen, you ain't going up dere to dat devil hole. It not be good for you."

"Nothing will happen, Tank. Is there a new key, Telemaque? If so I'd like to go up now."

"Yes, Miz Benoit," Telemaque said reluctantly, reaching into a drawer. "But don't expect nothing, it still being -"

"Remodeled. I know, Tel, these things take time, don't they?" She took the key from his shaky hand. "And don't you dare try to give me a gris-gris!"

"I go with she, gran'pere," Tank said bravely. "Me, I take care of Miz Karen real good."

"Go on, boy, you ain't been near dat place since -" he turned to Karen. "You *sure* you want to go up dere, Miz Benoit?"

"*Yes!* And by myself if you don't mind, Tank. The cook will wonder what happened to you."

Tank's eyes shone with relief. "Yeah, I better help dat old lady move dem boxes before she tan my hide." He ran backwards in the direction of the kitchen. "You come back soon, Miz Karen! Me, you, and Bo, we go fishing. Got me a new pole. Catch us beaucoup de catfish for a fish fry!"

"We'll go soon, I promise."

The boy crashed into a cuspidor in his backward dash, then limped off toward the kitchen. "Bye, Miz Karen!" he hollered over his shoulder. "Y'all come back!"

"I'll be back!" she called to his retreating back.

She walked to the elevator, stepped into the cage which once filled her with such dread, and pushed the button to the second floor.

# Chapter Thirty

During the slow journey upward, Karen thought of her therapist's diagnosis: "Manifestations of an agitated mind induced by guilt feelings and hallucinatory drugs." Psycho-babble was *her* diagnosis of his opinions. Anna, the cottage, her dreams, were lumped together as 'manifestations' produced, as she was repeatedly told, by an overactive mind. 'There were no ghosts. The images you saw were mere memories.'

Bullshit, she thought as she nodded in agreement, and he declared her cured.

Now she was back to learn the truth.

She stepped into the dark hallway and went surely to where the light switch was, flicked the switch and the hall was bathed in dim light. She waited for the nausea to begin again, the shock of cold sweat on her skin. Nothing. She walked to the new door of room 209 and inserted the key in the lock.

Nothing remained but the floor on which she stood and four charred black walls. The French doors had been replaced by boards and the balcony was gone. A musty odor of ashes permeated the room. Perhaps they would close the room forever and perpetrate the legend of the haunted hotel. Good advertising - if you didn't have to sleep in a haunted room.

She walks further into room 209 and calls softly. "Anna? Are you here?" The room is still. She feels a sense of waiting. Of melancholy. "Anna? I've come to say I'm sorry."

She spins about. Is that a whisper? A giggle? Is Anna back, ready to lure her again into her world of shadows and phantoms? Is Odette there? Young, silly, ready to play the wedding game once more? She hears nothing but the creak of a floorboard, a tired settling of the room. She waits for more, but the room is still.

She's disappointed. She wants to confront Anna; tell her she's sorry; try to befriend her again. For, in spite of what her therapist and a barrage of books had preached, Karen *knows* that she was served cookies and lemonade by her cousin in a little white house fifteen years after that cousin's death. She had gazed down upon a pitifully scarred face and later remembered the cause of its sadness.

Now she stands in the center of the room thinking of all that has happened, wondering what is to come.

She has Bo, all that really matters.

Doubt sets in. Had she really imagined it all?

Was she, after all, merely a would-be victim of an unbalanced woman wanting revenge for a terrible tragedy? No ghosts? No psychic phenomena?

She tries again.

"I returned your bracelet, Anna, it's back at the playhouse. I'm sorry for everything - the fire - your mother - were you there when she died? Did you see how it happened? I tried to save her but failed. Forgive me - and for the other. Your death. We were locked in during the fire. You know who locked the door. I escaped and you didn't. The simple truth is hard to accept."

She waits a moment, expecting - what? She desperately wants forgiveness, as she was able to forgive.

It is not meant to be. There is too much resentment.

She starts for the door, then is stopped by a gentle pressure on her arm, as light as the touch of a child, and a whisper like a soft breeze on a summer's day: "It's all right Karen. It wasn't your fault."

She bats back tears.

"Thank you, Anna, I accept your forgiveness. Goodbye, dear little cousin. I'm sorry for all that happened, but I won't be back."

Nothing more happens - no more caresses, no soft murmur reminding her of a kitten's purr. Did she imagine it? The touch, the whisper?

No, it wasn't a dream.

Bo waited for Karen in the lobby, his sweet kiss closing the door to room 209 forever.

As they drove to the security of Bo's gregarious Cajun family, Karen thought back on the picture that had changed her life: two little girls in a rowboat, smiling, full of life, their moment of happiness captured forever.

She was ready for that happiness.

CPSIA information can be obtained
at www.ICGtesting.com
Printed in the USA
FSOW02n2026200417
33384FS